The Gatekeeper
Paperback Copyright © 2022 Lorhainne Ekelund
Editor: Talia Leduc

ISBN-13: 9781998775248

Give feedback on the book at:
lorhainneeckhart@hotmail.com

Twitter: @LEckhart
Facebook: AuthorLorhainneEckhart

Printed in the U.S.A

The Gatekeeper

THE O'CONNELLS
BOOK SEVENTEEN

LORHAINNE ECKHART

About the O'Connells

The O'Connells of Livingston, Montana, are not your typical family. Follow them on their journey to the dark and dangerous side of love in a series of romantic thrillers you won't want to miss. Raised by a single mother after their father's mysterious disappearance eighteen years ago, the six grown siblings live in a small town with all kinds of hidden secrets, lies, and deception. Much like the contemporary family romance series focusing on the Friessens, this romantic suspense series follows the lives of the O'Connell family as each of the siblings searches for love.

The O'Connells

The Neighbor
The Third Call
The Secret Husband
The Quiet Day
The Commitment, An O'Connell Novella
The Missing Father
The Hometown Hero
Justice
The Family Secret
The Fallen O'Connell
The Return of the O'Connells
And The She Was Gone
The Stalker
The O'Connell Family Christmas
The Girl Next Door
Broken Promises
The Gatekeeper
The Hunted

**Seven years ago, she lost her husband.
Three years ago, her daughter was taken
from her.
Today, she's taking back her life.**

Being taken in by the O'Connells would be a bit overwhelming for some. But for Reine Colbert, the feeling of being on the outside, looking in is all too familiar. Yet when Suzanne O'Connell, the unruly rule-breaker, steps in with her very pregnant sister Karen to right all the wrongs Reine has suffered along the way, she exposes a deeply guarded secret involving crimes against other women, and the three soon find themselves in a perilous situation that could leave one of them paying the ultimate price.

CHAPTER

One

Reine woke to the sun streaming in, and she stretched before jolting upright, taking a second to realize where she was. She pressed her hand over her heart.

The window by her bed was open, with a light breeze fluttering the white cotton curtains. The double bed was comfortable, and she took in the white walls, the white metal bedframe, the wicker dresser with a mirror and a chair in the corner, and a small closet. The floral comforter on the bed reminded her of spring. The room was so welcoming, and the way the morning light danced off the walls was comforting. She still had to remind herself this was real.

Reine pulled in a breath and swept back her bed hair as she looked over to the bedside table, which had a digital clock. For a moment, she felt the familiar panic that had her tossing back the comforter, sliding her legs over the edge of the bed, and standing barefoot on the soft cotton throw rug. The clock said nine thirty-two. Reine couldn't believe she'd slept so late.

She stumbled over to the mirror, taking in her image and the long light green pajama T-shirt and shorts, which hung loose on her. They had been sitting on the bed for her—from Charlotte, she thought. She reached for a light blue housecoat on a hook on the back of the closed bedroom door, something else she thought Charlotte had put there for her, and turned the knob.

Her heart hammered with unwelcome unease as she stepped out, hearing a woman's voice downstairs. It was so quiet, and she wondered if she would ever find her footing. As she walked down barefoot, the creak of the stairs halfway had her jumping and staring for a second at the closed front door, the one she'd been on the other side of a few days earlier. That seemed like another lifetime now.

Reine pulled in one breath and then another, furious at herself for a second for being so jumpy. She forced herself to take another step down even though that irrational worry was still there, the worry that she could find herself thrown out the door and have her freedom yanked away again. She forced a swallow, willing her nerves to steady, as she heard the clatter of dishes and took in the short dark hair of a woman whose smile reached out to her.

"You're awake. Hope you slept well. Come on, sit. Coffee?" said Iris O'Connell, Marcus's mother, who had such a warm presence. Reine pulled out a stool at the island and sat beside two-year-old Cameron, who was in a high-back stool with a bowl of cereal and a cup of juice. He had dark hair with a natural wave, and she could see how much he looked like his father.

"I would love a coffee, thank you."

Iris filled a mug with big hearts on it. "Milk, sugar…?"

Reine shook her head. "Strong and straight, please."

Iris settled the steaming mug in front of her, and Reine lifted it, breathed in the coffee, which smelled heavenly, and took a swallow.

"This is good, thank you. Can't remember the last time I enjoyed a good cup of coffee." She glanced over to Cameron, who was staring at her, and back to Iris, who had her own mug of coffee and was now leaning on the island. "Eva's gone already, I guess. I wanted to be up and see her before she went to school." She didn't hear any other sounds in the house.

"You'll see her tonight. No one wanted to wake you. You had to be exhausted. Take some time, get some rest. Eva didn't want to go to school today; she wanted to stay home with you. Not sure how Marcus and Charlotte convinced her."

Reine took another swallow as she heard the front door open, and Suzanne walked in with her baby in a carrier.

"Hi, Reine…" she whispered. "I just got Arnie to sleep. He was fussy most of the night, up three times." She put the baby carrier right on the kitchen table behind her, and Reine took in the sleeping baby with a light blanket over him.

Suzanne walked right to the coffeepot and poured herself a coffee. "Harold had to work last night. Some call came in around two this morning. I'm sure it was the phone that woke the baby the second time right after I got him to sleep, so I took him to bed with me, and Harold never came home. He's going to be tired…" She had the fridge open and pulled out a plastic-covered plate of what she thought was leftover chicken from the night before, the barbecue.

This family seemed unusually close and so different in a way she didn't understand. She watched as Suzanne pulled out a piece and took a huge bite, and Iris only shook her head before taking the plate from her and putting it back in the fridge.

"Reine, how about some breakfast?" Iris said. "You have to be starving. I can whip you up some eggs and toast, or cereal…"

"Hey, and maybe Reine would like some leftover chicken? Not everyone eats cereal, Mom," Suzanne cut in after taking a big bite of meat from a thigh. She looked right at Reine. "I've never liked cereal. I'd just as soon heat up any leftovers from dinner in the fridge."

Iris shook her head and glanced up. Reine was really starting to get a picture of the dynamic of this family, Marcus and Charlotte's family, here in this house. She wondered when she wouldn't feel like an unwelcome guest.

"Eggs and toast, if it's not too much trouble," she said. Suzanne was still looking at her, unsmiling and unapologetic as she held that chicken thigh and chewed.

"It's no trouble at all, Reine," Iris said. "You live here now. You make yourself at home…" She moved Suzanne out of the way. There was something sweet about the teasing between them.

"That's right, because after today, you fend for yourself," Suzanne said. "I think we should put Reine in charge of side dishes for whatever Owen's barbecuing tonight. Did he seriously say tonight he wants fish?"

Reine didn't know what to say. She was stuck on the idea of her making a side dish. For what? She moved to lift her hand to ask, taking in the back and forth between mother and daughter, then pulled her hand down and decided to say nothing, trying to figure out what exactly they meant by "tonight."

"A friend of Owen's came back with a mess of trout, bull trout, or was it cutthroat?" Iris said to her before dragging her gaze back to Suzanne as if this were the most normal information to add to this odd conversation.

"Do you not remember the last time Owen barbecued cod, or was it salmon or something he picked up at the store? It was overcooked. He should stick to what he does best: burgers, chicken, or hotdogs. Or even pork chops. He hasn't done that in a while," Suzanne said before going on further about the fish.

Reine wondered whether they were talking about that night or a different night. She moved to raise her hand again.

"You have a lost look on your face over there, Reine. Everything okay?" Suzanne said. Meanwhile, Iris cracked eggs in a bowl before setting a fry pan on the stove and turning it on. Bread was in the toaster, as well.

"Well, I guess I don't understand," Reine said. "I'm supposed to come up with a side dish... Is this for a party? And Owen, your brother, is barbecuing? When? Is this at his place? I guess I don't understand what's going on. Maybe I'm just not clear on how everything works here. You look after Cameron? I take it Marcus and Charlotte are..."

Iris had poured the eggs from the bowl into the fry pan. Reine wasn't sure if that was an amused expression on her face.

Suzanne glanced her mother's way before looking

back to her. "Ah, I see you're trying to figure out how we all work. Well, we always have our noses in everyone's business. Family night happens…what, three or four times a week, usually? It's here, or at Ryan's, or at Mom's place, although with Tessa and Owen fixing up their little house and Chloe and Luke now living next door to them, I can see us starting to migrate more and more there. Harold and Arnie and I still live at his condo, which equals no house, no yard, and no barbecue." Suzanne took another bite of the chicken as Iris finished scrambling the eggs in the pan.

Reine was now starting to understand what Eva had said about family night. "So you basically have your own lives but are always together, and last night wasn't just because Marcus brought me back here?"

Suzanne was shaking her head as Iris scraped the eggs onto a plate and the toast popped up in the toaster. "Well, yeah, we were all waiting here to welcome you, but it's what we do. When she's in town, Mom looks after the kids, Cameron and Eva, either here or at her place, and when I get a job with the sheriff's department, Mom will also look after Arnie."

Iris rested the plate of eggs and buttered toast in front of Reine with a fork. "Here you go. Do you want peanut butter or jam on your toast?"

"Um, yeah, peanut butter would be great. Thank you. This is really nice…" She watched as Iris reached into the fridge and pulled out a jar of peanut butter, as well as a clean knife from a drawer, and slid them in front of her.

"Suzanne, you know Marcus already said no to a job at the sheriff's office," Iris said. "You really think you could work under him, considering the way you two butt heads? And do I need to remind you that your husband, Harold, is the lead deputy?"

Maybe it was hearing about the two men who'd arrested her that had Reine gripping the fork a little harder than she normally would have as she said, "Why do you want to be a cop?"

She hadn't meant to say it out loud. She glanced over to Cameron, who was eating with his hands now, picking the cereal out of his bowl, and she realized both women were staring at her. The moment had suddenly turned awkward.

"Well, for one, I loved being a first responder, but I got bounced out of that, and the current council here and the politics of the fire department have made sure I will never get hired here again. I think I would make a great cop, but Marcus keeps telling me no, he won't hire me."

Iris was looking at her as she slid her hand over the island. "You're still angry at Marcus?" she said. "I can see you're trying your best to hide the hurt. We could all see it last night, the tension that lingers between you and Marcus and Charlotte."

There it was, the eight-hundred-pound gorilla in the room, except neither was here. Yet she was under their roof, and she was still powerless even though she was free. "It doesn't go away overnight. I'm Eva's mother, but Marcus and Charlotte make all the decisions for her."

She hadn't meant to say that, either. After all, this was Marcus's family, closer than any she'd ever seen, and she was the outsider coming in.

"I understand, Reine, but know that you're welcome here," Iris said. "You're Eva's mother, and Eva is our family, and there is something about family, Reine. We fight, but we do forgive, eventually. You just need to find your footing. All I can say is just give it some time as you slip into this family. It's not all about their being in charge of Eva. It's about all of us. And Marcus feels horrible over what happened…"

"But I have no rights here." She wondered if she was smart or stupid for forcing her point. The awkwardness lingered again.

"You know what?" Suzanne said. "Finish up breakfast, and then get dressed. We're going out." She looked over to her mom. "Can you watch Arnie?"

She admired Suzanne and her determination. She wondered whether anything ever scared her.

"You know I will," Iris said.

"Okay, and where are we going?" Reine started as she reached for her fork again, feeling lost, not fitting in anywhere.

"It's a surprise, but it will do you good, give you a new perspective. Come on, finish up." Suzanne gestured at her plate, and Reine took in her bright smile.

Iris shrugged, looking back over to her. Just then, Cameron decided he was done, so Iris raced over and lifted Marcus's little boy, and Suzanne's baby started fussing from the car seat he was still in. Reine watched these two women she figured were trying to make her feel welcome. But, being the outsider, she still had no idea how she could fit into this family or what, exactly, her place was.

CHAPTER

Two

"I don't understand why you're being so nice to me," Reine said, speed-walking to keep up with Suzanne's long-legged stride.

"Excuse me? Seriously, Reine, you make me sound as if I'm tossing you a crumb, as if you're some charity case."

She wasn't sure what to make of Suzanne's remark or Suzanne, for that matter, as she took in the quaint downtown city block. The sun was out, but she was still fighting the urge to look over her shoulder.

"Here, put these on," Suzanne said as she reached into her bulky cloth purse and pulled out a baby soother, then a pair of polka-dot sunglasses. She tossed the soother back in her bag but stopped in the middle of the sidewalk until Reine took the sunglasses.

"Why…?" she said, but Suzanne had started walking again.

"Because of the way you keep looking over your shoulder with that spooked look on your face, as if you believe everyone knows your secret and wants to judge the shit out of you, look down on you, or maybe even spit on you. I see it and recognize it, as I've been there, so stop it and put them on."

She slid the sunglasses on and looked up at Suzanne as she hurried to keep up. "I don't think anyone would spit on me," she finally said in a low voice, wondering how Suzanne understood and had voiced what Reine believed deep inside herself.

"There you go. You just focus on that one positive thought. If anyone spits on you, I'd have to punch them, and then Marcus would show up and figure out a way not to arrest me."

There was something about Marcus's sister that Reine couldn't help but like. She even felt the tug of a smile at her lips. "You'd really slug someone?"

Suzanne made a rude noise as she stopped outside the door of a shop. Despite the noise of cars on the street and the chilly air, something felt so right about being with Suzanne.

"You have a beautiful smile, Reine," she said. "You should show it more. Yeah, I'd probably cause a scene, too. I've never been known to let anyone walk on me or anyone I care about. Oh, let's go in here." She pointed to a small store with a few mannequins displaying clothes in the window.

"Okay. So you haven't told me what the surprise is and where you're taking me." Reine followed Suzanne inside the store, which was filled with racks of clothes and the kinds of pretty things she couldn't afford. When was the last time she'd walked into a store like this? Damn, it had been a maternity shop in Denver when Eva was a baby and Vern was still alive. Just her and

Vern… The memory of his smile, his love, still cut so deep.

"Shopping," Suzanne said. "You need some clothes, because as cute as those worn jeans you have on are, they've seen better days. I think a few new things are a must."

She stopped just inside the front door when the irrational fear hit her, and she stared at Suzanne, who was at a rack of shirts, pulling one out. She wondered whether she'd lost her mind. The store clerk, unsmiling, was looking her way as she lifted her sunglasses and rested them on top of her head, which she'd only run a brush through. She stepped closer to Suzanne.

"Suzanne, I can't afford anything in here," she whispered, then realized the store clerk was listening to everything she said, so she turned her back on her, feeling uneasy.

"You don't even know how much anything is. Look, this is on sale for $19.99." Suzanne held up a shirt that Reine didn't look too closely at.

"If it costs anything, I can't afford it. I have no money," she said again in a low voice, wondering why Suzanne didn't know that.

"It's our treat, Reine. I talked with Mom, and I called Karen too, but it was Jenny who brought it up. We know you have nothing, so this is our 'welcome to the family' gift. Nothing I have will fit you, and the only one in the family who's close enough in size to you is Alison—and I doubt very much you would want anything Alison would wear, since it's all low-cut crop tops and skintight jeans."

Suzanne had her own sunglasses resting in her hair, the kind of brown that didn't stand out. She handed

Reine two shirts, a T-shirt with a cuddly cat on the front and a deep green blouse with flowers and short sleeves. "This is perfect for you, with your eyes."

Reine looked at the price tag, $39, and wondered if the strangled sound was from her. "This is too expensive, and where would I even wear it? It's too nice."

Suzanne handed her two more shirts and then walked over to a rack of blue jeans. Reine awkwardly gripped the hangers as Suzanne stared at her worn jeans before dropping her gaze to her feet and shaking her head.

"Nonsense," she said. "Just start trying things on, and we'll add some new shoes, too…"

"Can I help you two with anything?" said the clerk who'd been eyeing Reine since they walked in, standing right behind her. She had brown hair, wavy and thick, with mascara and mocha eyeshadow, and she wore a silky white sleeveless blouse, pumps, and trousers that looked like they cost a fortune. Reine was very aware of how she looked in comparison.

"Can you start a dressing room?" Suzanne said. "My friend here is getting an entire new wardrobe today."

Reine just stared at her.

"Of course I can. I'll put these in a room for you," the clerk said, looking at Reine as she reached for the shirts.

"Sure," was all she said in reply, and she wondered if the clerk was picking up on her unease.

Suzanne pulled out blue jeans and handed them over, then let her gaze land on Reine. "Any preference? High-rise, low-rise, sweaters, shirts, colors, or does it matter?"

Reine watched the saleslady walk away, then turned to Suzanne, who was staring at her again. "As you can see from the way I'm dressed, it doesn't matter. Clothes are clothes. Why are you doing this?"

Maybe she wasn't supposed to ask. Suzanne stilled, her hand on the rack, and took a second to look her way, no longer smiling. "Reine, I already told you we want to do this because you need clothes and because we can. It's what people who care do. And it's not as if we're dressing you for a dinner party. You can raid Alison's closet for that. This is just a small something. So just go try the clothes on. You're not signing your life away.

"This isn't charity, either, if that's what you think. It's our gift—which, by the way, if I have to say it again, you're going to have to get used to. We haven't had a chance to sit down and really talk. You've been stuck in a nightmare for so long, and your trust has been shattered, but just know you're in a safe place. We care. Just let that be enough right now. After you have your footing again, there will be a day one of us needs someone to pick us up, because we all do, and that will be your day to help, to be there for one of us."

God damn, how did she do that?

"Then we're going for lunch," Suzanne continued, "and that is my husband's treat."

Reine pulled in a breath, still feeling so damn nervous. "Okay, but don't go crazy."

There it was, the smile on Suzanne's face that she envied so much. Suzanne pulled out a black pair of jeans and handed them to her. "I swear. Just a few shirts, pants, and essentials, and you're set. Now go, try them on."

Reine squeezed the hanger and spotted the

curtained-off changing room in the back, feeling something she hadn't felt in a long time. As she stepped inside, where the clothes were hanging, waiting for her, she glanced back to Suzanne, who was now talking to the saleslady and handing her more clothes. Reine was still trying to figure out how it seemed her entire life as she knew it had changed overnight.

Three

"I've never heard her laugh before," Suzanne said as she walked into the kitchen, where Marcus and Harold were. "And look at her in there… Doesn't she look nice?"

Marcus only gestured with his beer toward Charlotte, who was chopping up peppers for a salad, and Suzanne still felt the unease lingering.

"She looks very nice, and Eva is happy, so that makes us happy," Charlotte said.

Harold was staring at Suzanne. She knew she was pushing it, but this awkward situation could have only one happy ending.

"You two have a chance to talk to her?" Suzanne continued.

There it was again, something in the exchange between Marcus and Charlotte. Her mom, who was holding Arnie, lifted a brow, and Suzanne could almost hear her warning her to stay out of the couple's business.

"Not yet," Charlotte said, "but we know we need to

settle some things. I think right now we're all in agreement that Eva lives here and so does Reine, at least until Reine gets back on her feet."

Marcus hadn't pulled his gaze from his wife, and Suzanne knew from the way Marcus was staring over at Charlotte that they might not be on the same page.

Harold pressed a kiss to Arnie's little hand as he took him from her mom, who then walked out of the kitchen. She listened to her baby's laugh, so new, but he could start fussing just as quickly. She heard the front door, then laughter from the living room, where Eva, Reine, Iris, Jenny, Alison, and her dad were. Ryan still hadn't shown up. Then there was Karen, whom she'd spoken with that morning.

"They had a case of assorted juice on sale, so I grabbed it," announced Owen as he stepped through the door, wearing his heavy jacket, with a five o'clock shadow, and Tessa followed him with a bright smile, her blond hair pulled back, carrying a paper bag. "Brady and Cassie aren't coming tonight. He's got some super-romantic thing planned for the two of them. Anyone hear from Luke or talk to Chloe?"

Suzanne wasn't sure what to make of Charlotte and Marcus. Unease, yes. She turned to the laughter from the living room. "Karen is supposed to be coming down tonight," she said. "I think she talked to Luke, and Chloe is coming later." Then, unable to take it anymore, she pressed her hand to the island and stared long and hard at Marcus and Charlotte. "Okay, you two, what's going on?"

Charlotte squeezed the knife and set it down, and Marcus finally pulled his gaze from her to look at Suzanne, annoyed. "Reine picked up Eva from school today, and no one thought to say anything to us," he said.

So there it was. Suzanne had overstepped in suggesting they pick her up. Iris had been onboard, but apparently Charlotte and Marcus hadn't. She hadn't expected this.

"Reine and I picked up Eva," she said. "I'm not sure how that's a problem, considering one of us always does…"

Owen was staring at Marcus, who shook his head and said, "It's not. It just surprised Charlotte, is all. We got a call from the school saying Reine had picked up Eva instead of Mom. They didn't mention you, Suzanne. This is all new, and we just have to figure it out and come to an understanding, with Reine living here now…" He kept his voice low, looking at Charlotte.

At a knock on the front door, Marcus frowned, and Suzanne stepped back to look through the screen, on the other side of which was someone she'd never seen before.

"Who is it?" Marcus said as he set his beer down on the counter and headed toward her.

"I don't know. Don't recognize him. You expecting someone?" Suzanne said, following him to the door, past Cameron, who came running into the kitchen toward Charlotte.

"Can I help you?" Marcus said as he pushed open the screen door with a squeak. She realized her dad was striding casually their way, his expression watchful.

"I'm looking for Reine Colbert."

She took in the man standing in the doorway, in a dark jacket and ball cap, of average height.

Marcus stood with one hand on the frame. "What is this about?" he asked.

Whoever this man was, Suzanne didn't recognize him, and she felt her brother's unease. The man was holding something, she thought.

"I've been given this address as hers. Is she here or not?"

Raymond glanced her way, standing off to the side, close to the door. Suzanne realized everyone had stopped talking. Reine was now walking their way in her new black jeans and navy shirt, her expression wary, her eyes big, on edge. Eva was holding her hand, staying close to her, something she did now.

Reine turned to her and leaned down. "Eva, it's okay. I'll be right back. Go to the living room with everyone. Nothing to worry about."

Eva stood there, looking far too worried. Damn, she was a smart kid, old enough to understand everything that was going on.

"Eva, come here," Iris called out from the living room.

"Why are you looking for Reine? Who are you?" Marcus asked the man again.

Reine walked past Suzanne to the door to stand beside him. Suzanne took another step closer, trying to see what was going on.

"I have something for Reine Colbert," the man said, his voice deep. "Are you Reine Colbert?"

"I am," Reine said in a low voice, and Suzanne wondered if anyone else could hear her uncertainty.

"You've been served," was all the man said in reply as he handed her a brown envelope. Then he left, and Suzanne took another step closer. Marcus stepped outside, and Ryan was striding up the steps, looking long and hard at the guy, whoever he was, as he hurried away down the sidewalk.

"What is it, Reine?" Suzanne said.

Reine's hands were shaking as she opened the envelope and pulled out the papers, then let out a heavy sigh. "I don't know. I'm being sued." She tapped the papers. "I don't understand. It's about Vern…"

Suzanne looked over her shoulder, trying to read all the fine print.

"Reine, can I take a look at that?" Raymond asked. He had a way about him, not taking over the situation but simply being kind, compassionate, watchful. She realized he didn't miss anything.

"Sure…" Reine handed him the papers.

Marcus and Ryan stepped inside and closed the door.

"What was that about?" Ryan asked. Suzanne gave him only a passing glance as she looked over to her dad, who was reading the papers. He lifted the first page and shook his head.

"They're coming after you for unpaid medical bills, and then there are back taxes owing for Vern Colbert. With interest on interest, this is close to four million."

Suzanne wasn't sure if that strangled sound was from her or Reine. She turned back to see Harold walking closer, handing over Arnie to Tessa. On instinct, Suzanne rested a hand on Reine's shoulder. Everyone was now listening, standing. The energy had ramped up.

"Are you kidding? Why? How is this possible?" Suzanne said, very aware of how quiet Reine had become, aware of everything she'd lost. How could they be coming after her still?

"They took everything from me, and now they want four million more? It was never that much, but it was still too much. They took our house. I sold everything I had, and every paycheck I had went to them. How is this possible? My husband is dead, yet it's just never-ending bullshit…" She reached for the papers, and Raymond gave them back.

"It looks like interest at rates I've never seen before, with tax on top of it," he said.

Marcus had his arms crossed, staring down at Reine, who was now reading all the fine print, gripping the papers so hard. Damn, she was just getting kicked over and over.

"We'll give it to Karen," Suzanne said. "She can go over it. This is so wrong, but, Reine, don't worry. Maybe this is a good thing…"

Everyone was looking at her, and the horror in Reine's eyes had her wanting to shut her mouth and backtrack.

"A good thing?" Reine spat out.

"I didn't mean it that way. They're coming after you even though they've already screwed you and your husband, so how about fighting back?"

Evidently, no one understood what she was trying to say.

"Maybe Reine isn't a pit bull like you are, Suzanne," Marcus added.

Reine still said nothing.

There were times she wanted to pull Marcus aside, like now, and remind him that rolling over was never the answer. She wondered when he'd become so cautious.

"Look, this heavy-handed crooked shit from this goliath is garbage. Reine, you lost everything because of these guys, and now they've decided they want to take another chunk out of you? Say no. Stand up. We can fight this."

"How am I going to fight it? Now they want more, and I'll never be able to pay. I don't understand. Seven years ago I lost my husband, and they took my house, my bank account, my job, my life. How can they keep doing this?" Reine's eyes were wide, and the emotion in her voice cut Suzanne deep.

"That's what they want, Reine, to cripple you," Raymond said. "But Suzanne is right. It's a game to them, and because they're as big as they are, it has made them untouchable, allowing them to take from vulnerable, hardworking families and destroy them because they can't and don't fight back. They may as well ask for ten million or twenty. It doesn't matter, because they won't get it. Have Karen look at it. They're just trying to scare you, is all. You paid how much to them? I don't know everything, Reine, only what Iris told me about what happened…"

Suzanne touched Reine's shoulder again, feeling how tense she was. She didn't know what she was thinking as she stared at the papers.

"Karen is due to have the baby anytime," Marcus said, cutting in. "This probably isn't the time to put this on her plate."

Suzanne dragged her gaze over to her brother, wanting to kick him. "Her sharp legal mind still works, pregnant or not, and she's not due for another five weeks. Should I tell her you didn't want to bother her?" she tossed right back at him, knowing Karen would come out swinging, especially when she found out

Marcus had tried to coddle her. She didn't know why her brother had said that.

Ryan was quiet, as was Reine, and she looked back to see Eva watching and listening—upset and scared, maybe.

"I don't have money to pay Karen…"

"Nonsense," Suzanne said. "This isn't about money. This is family, Reine. Have Karen take a look into this. It could be a clerical error, because it happens." She shrugged at the way everyone was looking at her. "Well, it's true. Bureaucracy at its finest."

Reine tucked the papers back into the envelope and lifted her gaze to Marcus first, then to Ryan and then over to Suzanne. "Sorry to ruin the evening. I'm going to put this away," she said, then stepped around Suzanne and started up the stairs.

The lingering quiet only added to the unease. Suzanne wanted to slug Marcus as she gestured to where Reine had disappeared at the top of the stairs. Above them, a door opened and then closed.

"'Don't put this on Karen's plate…' Are you serious, Marcus?" She stepped toward him, then felt her dad touch her shoulder.

Marcus made a rude sound and ran his hand over the back of his head. "Look, I didn't mean we wouldn't help." He gestured to her. "It's just I know how Jack feels right now. He doesn't want unnecessary stress on Karen. Did you forget about her miscarriage? That's the only reason I said it."

His words felt like a slap, but she knew her sister was a born fighter, just like her.

"We'll all help," Raymond said in a low voice,

maybe to remind them of how loud they were. "But now isn't the time. Right now, Eva is listening."

Suzanne turned back to see her mom standing maybe ten feet back with her hand on Eva's shoulder. The expression on her little niece's face was the same one Suzanne had seen nearly three years earlier when her world had fallen apart, when her mom had been taken from her and she had come to live with Marcus and Charlotte.

"Is that about my dad?" Eva said.

Suzanne felt the ache in her chest. Damn, she was smart.

"Yeah," Marcus said, walking around Suzanne and toward his adopted daughter, running his hand over his head again. "But you know what, Eva? It's going to be fine. We're going to handle it…" He somehow maneuvered Eva back into the living room just as Arnie started fussing.

Ryan shrugged out of his coat, and Owen walked out the back door to the barbecue. Charlotte was holding Cameron, but she was looking at Suzanne and then at the stairs. As she turned away and walked back into the kitchen, Suzanne felt something she had sensed before, that something was simmering beneath the surface. She had a feeling Reine was not as welcome in their home as Charlotte had said.

Four

Reine pulled at the thick blue sweater Suzanne had bought her as she sat on the stool at the island in the kitchen. Hearing the creak of the floorboards, she sat up to see Marcus. It was dark, and only the light over the stove was on.

"I didn't know you were down here," he said. "What are you doing up?" He wore a T-shirt and sweatpants, and he walked over to the sink and leaned against it.

"Sorry, couldn't sleep and figured I'd read through this…" She lifted the papers she'd been served with. Reading the legalese, the dollar amounts, she was having a hard time understanding how this had suddenly ballooned into something she'd never be able to pay back.

Marcus crossed his arms. She was still uneasy with him and wondered if she would ever feel differently. She lowered her gaze back to the papers, maybe because of how he was looking at her.

"Look, I'm sorry this was brought to your doorstep," she said.

He let out a heavy sigh. "Don't apologize. That isn't your fault. I can see how this rattled you."

She never knew what to make of Marcus and what he really thought of her. Did he hate her? She didn't have a clue how to read him. She sat a little straighter, pulling her sweater closed over her lightweight pajamas, feeling the chill on her bare feet. The way he looked at her unsettled her at times, but he didn't look away, so she only nodded and pressed her hand to the papers.

He walked over to the island. "You mind if I have a look?" He reached out, and she glanced back to the papers, which were like an anvil that would forever be hanging over her.

"Okay, I guess." She pushed them across the island and Marcus reached for them and leaned down, one hand resting on the countertop, the other lifting the second page. It was so awkward, and she should have been embarrassed, but she no longer had any secrets Marcus didn't know.

"This is from a collection company for the hospital and, it appears, the IRS. It's a demand for $4,087,989.89, right to the penny, for treatment and taxes. I see most of it is interest. Did you talk to Karen?" He flicked those O'Connell blue eyes over to her, and in the dim light, she made out something else there. Sympathy, maybe?

She shook her head. "No, I don't feel right calling Karen. She's already done so much for me…"

Marcus was shaking his head as he set the papers down. "Call her. Suzanne is right; she's our family lawyer, and she'd be mad if you didn't. She could likely make one call and get this sorted out. Do you mind if I ask you something personal?"

She didn't know what to say. She took in the ring on his finger, knowing his wife was upstairs, a woman who loved her daughter so much. She wasn't a fool. She knew Charlotte really didn't want her there.

"No, I guess not." She flicked her gaze to the papers still in front of Marcus, very aware it was now after midnight.

"Vern, your husband, when did the insurance company deny coverage for him? It was lung cancer he had?"

She didn't think she'd ever forget the day she'd walked through the doorway of their small house in Missoula to find him sitting in a corner of the living room, too quiet. She'd known at once that something was wrong.

"Yes, a rare form, apparently, but one that's all too common for firefighters. Eva was only six months old. They didn't deny coverage for him right away. He saw an oncologist and did radiation first, then drugs and chemo, which didn't work but made him so sick. There was an experimental drug they wanted to try that had been successful in other cases, only the cost was ridiculous. Each day was horrible with worry, but I never thought the insurance company would come back to the doctor to say they weren't going to cover a treatment they considered experimental, even though it had been used thousands of times. The doctor said that was happening more and more.

"What were our options? This was my husband. Of course I knew there was no choice. The hospital agreed to go ahead. We were on the hook for those treatments, and three weeks before Vern died, a letter arrived in the mail, saying they were denying all coverage and coming after us for what had already been paid because of a pre-existing condition."

Marcus was so quiet. Reine had never been able to talk about what had happened without feeling the absence where the giant ache had once been.

"He was a fireman," he said, "breathing in toxic chemicals, running in and out of burning buildings. Even I know cancer is the biggest killer of firefighters."

She only nodded, remembering his dark hair, which had grown back, his blue eyes, and his disbelief when he read what the insurance company had found out. "When Vern was fifteen, he smoked, if you can call it that, for a few months, horsing around with friends. It was in the letter. They cited a clause in the health coverage contract that no sane person would have been able to find. A pre-existing condition? It was ludicrous, and how did they find out, considering even his parents never knew?" Maybe that was what bothered her more than anything. "I mean, how could they uncover something like that unless they took his life apart, our lives? They must have spent so much on investigators to go back and dissect his past, talk to his childhood friends. It's unbelievable, if you think about it."

Marcus glanced over his shoulder and then back to her. "Unfortunately, insurance companies have resources the average person will never have, and they can uncover things even I would never be able to." Marcus pointed to the paper again. "Call Karen in the morning. Or do you want me to?"

She and Marcus had never really had time to talk before, but there was something calming about speaking with him when Charlotte wasn't around. "I'll call her, thanks." She had to force a smile to her face, as it suddenly felt so awkward.

"I'm sorry, Reine. Eva never got to know her father."

She sat up straight. "Eva didn't have much of a childhood. He died five days before her second birthday. I think that letter from the insurance company took the final piece out of him. They took our house, my dignity, my family, my joy, and they still want more." She tried to force a smile as Marcus walked around the island and rested his hand on her shoulder.

"Well, how about it's time you take it back? What they did was wrong. I haven't offered you any advice, so I hope you'll be okay with me putting this out there, but after Karen puts this to rest, you should consider burying them. Go after them for everything they took from you for denying coverage because they could. There's one thing I know well, Reine: When you deal with giants like this, the government, insurance companies, they don't play fair, and they don't go after people who can fight back."

This was something else she hadn't expected from Marcus.

"I'm going to bed," he finally said. "You'll be okay?" He looked down at her, and there was something about this man who had taken her child in, adopted her, and opened his door to her.

"I'll be fine. I'm not far behind. Can I ask you something?"

Marcus had taken only a few steps, and he turned around. For a moment, the tension she'd always felt seemed to have disappeared. "Okay," he said. There was a smile. He really did have a nice smile.

"You sure it's okay that I'm here?" she said.

"It's not a question, Reine. Of course it is. You're Eva's mother."

It wasn't really the answer she was looking for, but she wondered whether he understood what she was getting at.

"I know that, Marcus, but have you asked Charlotte? Because she's your wife, and this is her house too."

He only looked away. There it was again, the tension. "Don't worry about Charlotte. And call Karen in the morning. Goodnight," he said. Then he walked away, and she listened to his footsteps on the stairs.

She thought of the woman who'd adopted her daughter. She wasn't a fool. No matter what Charlotte said, she knew she didn't really want her there, and she definitely didn't want her to have any say in how she raised her daughter.

Marcus stepped out of the bedroom, tucking in his shirt and fastening his duty belt. Charlotte was already dressed, holding Cameron as she walked into Eva's bedroom and called out, "Come on, Eva, get dressed now! …Oh, didn't know you were in here, Reine. Good morning. Did you sleep well?"

Cameron fidgeted, and Charlotte put him down. He raced off past her when he heard a key in the front door, knowing that had to be his grandma.

"Hey, slow down there, bud…" Marcus said, but his son was already running down the stairs. Marcus went down the top two steps in time to see Cameron leap at his mom. Then he started down the rest of the way.

"Wow, haven't even made coffee yet," he said. "How are you this morning, Mom?"

"It's chilly out. You can feel the snow in the air. I think it'll be a cold one this winter…" She looked up to the stairs, and Marcus heard footsteps and turned to see his wife. Her usual smile was missing. Cameron was already in the kitchen, and he'd be on the counter in a second, likely yanking out the only cereal he would eat as of late, Oaty O's.

Maybe his mom picked up on Charlotte's off-ness, as she gave him an odd glance as she reached the bottom step.

"Reine is insisting on helping Eva get dressed," Charlotte said, an edge in her voice, though he didn't understand the problem. She kept walking into the kitchen, and he followed her, but Iris touched his arm to stop him.

"I thought everything was okay here with Reine?" she said, her voice just above a whisper. What was he supposed to say? Charlotte had been okay until, apparently, she wasn't.

He only shook his head and kept walking to the kitchen, where Charlotte was lifting Cameron off the counter with the box of cereal. "Go sit down," she told him, gesturing.

Iris stepped in and took the bowl from Charlotte as Marcus lifted Cameron onto the stool at the island. Milk was poured on his cereal, and Charlotte was quietly making coffee. Then she was in the fridge, pulling out butter and eggs. She reached for the bread and put two pieces in the toaster.

"And what's wrong with Reine helping Eva?" Marcus said. "I think you help her pick out clothes to wear more days than not. Reine missed a lot with her. I don't see why it's a big deal."

He felt the nudge in his side, and when he looked over to her, his mom made a face as if he'd said something he shouldn't.

"I know she did, but she's overstepping, and maybe

this makes me sound cruel, but Eva is ours. I'm her mother. She's…"

He could see how tense she was, feeling the moment this could go sideways. Cameron was shoving cereal in his mouth, already dripping milk on his light brown shirt. Marcus found himself looking up, listening, knowing mother and daughter were both upstairs.

"Charlotte, we talked about this," he said. "You were onboard with having Reine here. Are you telling me you don't want her here now?"

She reached for a fry pan and set it on the stove, then pressed both palms to the island. She was tense, and he couldn't remember the last time he'd seen her so off. He felt for a second as if he were wading into dangerous territory. Maybe his mom knew, as she pressed her hand to his arm again. Cameron looked up to him too, his mouth full, chewing around the cereal.

"I don't, Marcus," Charlotte finally said. "Even saying it, I feel horrible, but I feel like I'm competing with her. I know Reine is Eva's mother, but so am I. We're her parents now, and we're the ones who are raising her, making decisions for her, not Reine. Yet every time I turn around, there she is with Eva. Yesterday, showing up at the school and picking her up, that was too much. I mean, what if one day she just disappears with her?"

For a moment, Marcus didn't know what to say. He found himself taking in how quiet his mom was, linking her hands together. He looked down to his son again, who was more interested in shoving food in his mouth than in the conversation.

"Well, Charlotte, I may be overstepping," Iris said, "but don't we all pick her up from school? If not me, it's

Suzanne, and even Owen and Tessa did it twice just last week. Jenny and Alison, too. I don't see the issue, Charlotte. In fact, I told Suzanne it was a great idea when she called. Are you asking for all of us to clear it with you?"

He hadn't expected that from his mom, and he could see the moment Charlotte regretted everything she'd said. She pulled her lower lip between her teeth, shut her eyes, and pressed her hand to her forehead. Then she looked over to them.

"No, of course not," she said. "I'm sorry. I know it's irrational, but I feel that…"

"She's competing with you for Eva's love," his mom cut in.

He heard footsteps and the excitement in Eva's voice even though he couldn't make out what they were saying.

"Okay, maybe I sound ridiculous," Charlotte said. "I shouldn't have said it."

He just stared, wondering why she would think that, just as Reine and Eva walked in, the image of mother and daughter, a bond no one could break.

"Wow, look at you today in all yellow," Marcus said. Eva let go of her mom's hand, and he took in Reine, who wore a blue and white blouse and blue jeans. The unease was still there. A coffee appeared on the island in front of him.

"Reine, coffee?" Charlotte said in a much lighter tone.

Reine shook her head. "Sure, but you don't have to wait on me. I know you both have to get to work. I wanted to say something first: Thanks for letting me stay. I'm going to call Karen this morning. And thanks for the words of encouragement last night, Marcus. It helped."

He reached for his coffee and could feel Charlotte staring his way. "Let me know how it goes with Karen," he said. "In fact, I'll be talking to her later…"

"Well, Karen is already here," Iris said. "She and Jack arrived late last night. They're at the condo. I was going to go over after I drop off Eva at school and take this ball of energy with me." She rustled Cameron's dark hair.

He found himself looking over to Charlotte, who was pouring coffee in two mugs. She handed one to Reine and the other to his mom.

"Why don't you tag along, Reine?" Iris said. "You can help me with this guy, and then you and Karen can talk."

It was a great idea, but he didn't know what to make of the way Charlotte had turned as the toast popped up.

"Does anyone want eggs?" she said. "I can put them on, or…"

Yup, she was flustered, off.

"Toast is good," Marcus said, "but we need to get going."

Reine set her coffee on the island, walked around it, and said, "Charlotte, why don't you let me butter the toast?"

For a second, he didn't know what Charlotte would say. He took another swallow of his coffee. Then Charlotte put down the knife and slid over the butter. "Sure, that would be great," she said. "You know what? I forgot something upstairs."

She walked out of the kitchen, her smile tight, and then over to the stairs. When Marcus looked back, Reine was buttering the toast, and his mom had pulled out peanut butter and honey.

Charlotte was now upstairs, and unless he figured out a way to get her to understand that it wasn't a competition for Eva, he figured the tension and awkwardness could make things difficult for all of them.

"Excuse me," he said, having finished off the last of his coffee. "Have a good day at school, Eva, and you behave yourself for Grandma." He rustled both kids' hair and took in how comfortable Reine was with his mom. Then he started over to the front door and looked up the empty stairs, realizing this thing with Charlotte could quickly get out of hand.

He listened to Eva's laughter, the voices from the kitchen, and then glanced to the top of the stairs again, where Charlotte was now looking down at him. There was something he'd never thought he'd see in the face of the woman he loved. She couldn't hide how much she didn't want Reine there.

"Hey, Marcus, you got a second?" Harold said to Marcus as soon as he walked through the door of the station behind his wife, who was still very much out of sorts. She headed right to her desk, and Harold flicked his gaze over to her. He never showed what he was thinking, but he had evidently picked up on how off Charlotte was.

"Sure, come on in," Marcus replied as he walked into his office. He shrugged out of his coat with the sheriff's logo on it and put it on the coat rack, very aware of the silent treatment from his wife. He knew this was dangerous territory, filled with landmines, yet he didn't have a clue what he was supposed to have figured out.

"Thought you would want to know I had some feelers put out about Manny Meskill," Harold said. "You wanted me to do some digging into his personal life—well, if you can call it that. He's apparently not what you would call a highly respected parole officer, but because of his years on the job and his seniority, he does what he does and no one looks his way or questions anything. He is divorced three times, with two grown children he hasn't seen in years, and he's never had a complaint against him that stuck. One Susan Peters accused him of assaulting and robbing her, but she later retracted it, and it isn't in any official records. I found out from a clerk I know in the DA's office. But I was told something rather interesting: No one is stupid enough to cross Manny, and it isn't uncommon for his female parolees to suddenly have additional time tacked on."

Now that had his attention. He sat on the edge of his desk just as Charlotte walked in with a coffee and held it toward him.

"Seriously? And no one's questioned that?" he said, then took the coffee. "Thanks, Charlotte."

She only nodded, but she was still standing there. Apparently, she had something on her mind, and maybe Harold realized it.

"No one," he said. "They're ex-cons, so no one is looking at how they're being treated."

"But you said it's all women, not any of the men?" He took a swallow of the hot coffee and dragged his gaze over to Charlotte, who had pulled her hands tight across her chest and pulled her lips between her teeth. She was really tense, and he wasn't sure he wanted to hear what she had to say. He looked back over to Harold.

"No men," he said. "Just women, from what I was able to find. Not all of them, but enough that it has me wondering, so I think tonight I'm going to follow him and watch him, see where he goes, what he's up to."

Marcus nodded, picturing what Meskill had done to Reine. Yet she was the source of his wife's self-imposed misery. "You know what?" he said. "I think I might handle this one myself."

Harold looked over at Charlotte, then shrugged. "Sure. You want me to keep looking into him?"

Marcus listened to Charlotte's heavy sigh and flicked his gaze to his coffee. "Yeah, keep digging. I want to know who he sees, who his friends are, where he spends his free time, where he banks. Turn over every rock. I'll put a tail on him tonight and see what I can see."

Harold said nothing else, just walked out of the office, and Charlotte closed the door behind him. Her hand was still on the handle when she turned, evidently getting ready to say something he might not want to hear.

"What's up, babe?" He did his best to put all the compassion he could in his voice.

"I want her out of our house." She was walking right toward him, and the way she said it, he could see how close she was to snapping.

"You want who out of our house? I hope you're not talking about Reine." He stared down at his coffee again. Charlotte was really struggling, and when she looked over to him, he could see tears in her eyes now, something he hadn't expected.

"Hey, what's going on?" He put his coffee down and walked over to her, and when she put her hand to her face and sniffed as a tear slid down, Marcus rested his hands on her shoulders.

"I'm not a cruel person, Marcus." She flicked her gaze up to him. He could see now that this wasn't sitting well with her.

"I know you're not, but you can't seriously be talking about throwing Reine out?"

It was there in her expression. "I am, and I know it sounds horrible, but I never expected to feel like a guest in my own house. Eva is ours. We adopted her. Reine is no longer her mother. I am. Yet every time I turn around, there she is with Eva, in her room in the morning, sitting on her bed, brushing her hair or picking out clothes with her, putting a puzzle together with her, making a sandwich for her. I turn around and ask Eva to put away her clothes or fold the laundry, and you know what she did yesterday? She looked to Reine to see if it was okay. Reine! The woman has no right to be saying anything to Eva."

He let his hands fall away and wondered how she could see what he didn't.

"Reine is not undermining you. You and I talked about this, and you were on board with having her move in after what happened to her. You know what it did to Eva. Let me ask you what would happen if we told Reine to move out. You think Eva would be okay with that? Because I don't. As a matter of fact, she'd hate us, and I'm not doing that to her. After what those two have been through, and now with her getting served last night by the same overreach that put her and Eva on the street, that would be the same as turning our backs on her. Is that what you want, to kick Reine to the curb?"

Charlotte squeezed her fists and moved in a circle away from him, running her hand over her forehead and her dark hair, which was pulled back in a ponytail. "I need you to back me up, Marcus."

There he was again, crossing the minefield.

"I always back you, Charlotte. You know that. But I'm not asking Reine to leave. She has nothing. Her spending time with Eva is the only reason she's here, and the fact is that she's Eva's mother. We may have adopted her and are her legal guardians, but you cannot change the fact that Reine is her biological mother. What do you want her to do, not spend time with Eva? Or is it that you're looking for her to check in with you before she does anything with her? I think you know my mom, my sisters, even Jenny and Tessa have stepped in with the kids. They don't ask. Why is it different with Reine?"

Charlotte was staring at him with a lingering heaviness. He could see she had her mind made up. "It is different, Marcus, and how it's different is that your family has never disrespected me. There is an understanding of boundaries, a mutual respect…"

So that was it. "You don't think she respects you?" he said. He was trying to figure out how Reine had disrespected her when what he'd seen had been exactly the opposite.

"Of course she doesn't," she said. "And what did she mean about thanks for last night?"

He didn't want this going on under their roof. He wanted to laugh, but the way she was looking at him, he knew that wouldn't be smart. "Nothing, it means nothing. I went downstairs, thought I heard something after midnight, but it was just Reine in the kitchen, sitting there, buried in those damn papers. I took a minute to read them and offered my opinion and our help, is all. I can only imagine the stress that's been added to her, and I seriously hope we can do something."

Charlotte crossed her arms over her chest, under her full breasts, pulling at the buttons of her brown deputy shirt. He realized she wasn't really seeing Reine the way he was.

"You know," he said, "you, me, and Reine do need to sit down and talk."

"I need you to be on my side, Marcus, not Reine's."

He stared at his wife, realizing he wasn't convincing her of anything. "I don't know what that means, Charlotte. You're my wife, I love you, and I'm not taking her side. But you need to ease up on her. She's trying to find her footing. You should know she's already picked up on the fact that you don't like her. Maybe you two should sit down together. Talk to her and be the compassionate woman I love. This isn't a contest for Eva's love. There's enough to go around. I don't know how this is going to work, but you agreed this was the right thing, and this is for Eva."

Charlotte made a face, and he thought just maybe he was getting through to her.

"She had the shit kicked out of her," he said. "How about just getting to know her? She's not trying to fill your shoes, but you can't fill hers, either."

"I know that," she snapped.

"Then explain this to me. Are you wanting her to ask your permission before she goes into Eva's room, talks to her, plays a game with her…?" He knew how much Charlotte loved Eva, yet the tension was becoming too thick in the house.

"No, of course not. I just want Reine to understand that I'm Eva's mother and make the decisions for her, not her. She lost that right."

Marcus angled his head at the hard line his wife was taking. "You want to grind her into the ground and have her answer to you, is that what this is? Don't you think she's had enough of that? This is a complicated situation, and it isn't about our family anymore—you, me,

Cameron, and Eva. Reine is now part of it. She had her rights ripped away, but she's a good woman. Put yourself in her shoes, Charlotte. Every decision she made, every choice… How would you feel if Eva were Cameron, and you were suddenly a guest in someone's house, seeing someone else raising your child and trying to find your place in your own child's life? Don't look at me like that, because I can see you're ready to go a few rounds with Reine, and I'm telling you, don't do it. Because if you do, you will lose Eva. Make it work, Charlotte. Find a way to make her part of the family."

She turned her head, fisting her hands, her arms crossed tight. "Fine, I won't say anything. But I won't have Reine challenging me, Marcus."

He let out a heavy sigh. There was a point where Charlotte became unreasonable and couldn't be convinced of anything.

"And I don't want her picking Eva up from school anymore," she said.

He put his hands on his duty belt and glanced down. "So is this where you tell Mom she can't pick up Eva either, or Suzanne, or Jenny, or maybe my brothers?" He knew it had come out rather sharply.

"That's different, Marcus." She leaned in, and he could see she wasn't hearing anything from him.

"No, it's not, Charlotte. You're picking a fight with a woman who has been drowning for so long. You were onboard with having her move in, and now you want to rip her world apart, and Eva's? The fact that you can't see that should bother you."

Charlotte stepped back and held her hands up, putting distance between them. "You know what,

Marcus? I'm your wife. You're supposed to back me." Her hand was now on the door.

"I love you, Charlotte, but I'm not kicking a woman to the curb because you want me to."

She pulled open the door and went to step out, her back stiff with the kind of tension he'd never felt before. "You can sleep on the sofa," she said. Then she stepped out of his office.

He lifted his gaze to the ceiling, seeing the faded white, and for the life of him, he had no idea how to get his stubborn wife to see reason.

"You sure you don't want anything in your coffee?" said the governor of Montana, Jack Curtis, as he held out a coffee to Reine where she sat on a plush green sectional.

"Just black," she said. "Thank you. I appreciate this."

He really was a handsome man, dressed in dark pants and a light blue shirt minus a tie. His smile reminded her of Vern in a way. The man oozed power, and she was well aware that her freedom was because of him.

He only nodded as she took the large green mug, hearing Iris in Karen's kitchen with a rambunctious Cameron, who was pushing a big toy Tonka truck around the small two-bedroom condo.

"This is absolute bullshit," Karen said from where she was sitting in a leather easy chair. "I don't even know where to begin. Damn, I have to pee again…" She struggled to slide forward, setting the legal papers on the table beside her, and Jack was right there, helping his very pregnant wife up. She was short, just like Iris and Reine, and maybe that was why she appeared as if she could go into labor any day.

There was a knock at the door, and Jack walked over and pulled it open to reveal Suzanne and her baby in a carrier, accompanied by one of the state troopers who followed the sitting governor everywhere.

"Hey, Reine," Suzanne said. "Thanks, Jack. I see you have the entire three-ring circus here. How do the residents of the condo feel with state troopers on the floor?"

Exactly the same thing that Reine had wondered the moment they'd stepped into the building and off the elevator. It was unnerving for her, but likely not in the same way it was for everyone else. Her hands were still sweating, but at least her heart wasn't slamming in her chest from the way the trooper at the door stared at her. She reminded herself he was just doing his job, but she would likely always see every cop as someone who would hurt her.

"It goes with the territory, Suzanne. It would help if Karen would sell this place, but she insists we come back here far more often than my security is comfortable with," Jack said. Then he said something to one of the troopers, who pulled the door closed.

Reine lifted her mug and took a swallow, watching as Suzanne made herself at home and set Arnie, who was sound asleep in his baby carrier, in the middle of the coffee table right in front of her.

"Oh, that feels better. Sorry about that," Karen said as she waddled back in, wearing maternity pants and a bulky pink T-shirt. Her hair, a mix of red and blond, was pulled back. She slowly made her way back to sit down in the chair, and she hissed, looking uncomfortable.

"You okay?" Jack said, hovering, concerned. For a moment, Reine wondered if maybe he was angry that she was there with her problems.

Karen lifted her hand to wave him off. "Just uncomfortable with having to pee every ten minutes, it seems. Stop hovering. Suzanne, thought you'd have been here an hour ago."

Suzanne wasn't smiling, only shaking her head. "Long night with the baby. He was up three times, so he'd better stay asleep." She flicked her gaze down to the carrier.

"Well, you're here now," Karen said. "And you're right about this, Suzanne. This is absolute bullshit, this insurance company and the IRS coming after Reine. They're doing this to you because they can. You know, I would not hesitate to estimate that the number of lives they've ruined is massive. They would never pull this on anyone who could fight back. One letter from one good lawyer and they'll be running the other way. I guarantee you, Reine, that they investigated you and Vern before they pulled this and likely hedged their bets that you wouldn't and couldn't fight back."

Karen was holding the papers up again, and she flicked her blue eyes, which held a fire and passion that Reine so admired, over to her and then to Suzanne. "Marcus really said not to bother me because I'm too pregnant?"

Suzanne rocked the carrier a couple of times when Arnie appeared as if he were about to wake up. Then she stepped back, shrugged out of her coat, and tossed it on the end of the sectional. "He did. Can you believe it?"

The way Suzanne said it, Reine felt as if the sisters were ready to tar and feather their brother. She was still struggling to find her way in the dynamics of this family. Iris, their mother, had a boyfriend they called Jake, but the way everyone reacted to him and treated him, she had a feeling he was something more. Eva had even begun to let something slip that morning about who Jake was before clamming up. She felt that this family had secrets.

"Oh, I can believe it, and I'll be setting him straight," Karen said. She was a woman who didn't let anyone tell her what to do.

Reine found herself looking over to Jack as she reached over to the carrier and kept rocking Arnie for Suzanne, as she could see he would wake up screaming if the rocking stopped.

"How about you just not, Karen?" Jack said.

There was another knock at the door, but Karen didn't seem to notice, and Reine didn't know where to look.

"Okay, first things first, Reine," Karen started. "Suzanne is right about a few things. This insurance company is one of the biggest on the west coast. They have influence with hospitals and doctors over their protocols, which drugs they use, which procedures. It's something the average person would never believe, but this is what happens when billion-dollar companies have too much power. They hold the purse strings that keep hospitals afloat, pay doctors' salaries, and fund research on drugs. They all hold shares in pharmaceuticals, too. Damn, I hate these guys.

"Firefighters have the highest cancer rates. Your husband being declined a drug and then you becoming responsible for the medical cost should be criminal and is morally wrong, but unfortunately, it's completely legal because of the power these companies have. They control the laws. I've told my husband he's got to rescind so many of these bills and executive orders that have given a free ride to these guys."

Reine found herself looking over to Jack, who was now back in the open kitchen on the other side of the island with Iris. She didn't know what to make of his expression.

"Karen, you know the state legislature can overturn anything I do," he said. "And the process is a long one, with too many players involved. For-profit hospitals operate under different laws than state and federal hospitals, so it isn't possible for me to make an executive order that private insurance companies cannot deny claims. It wouldn't hold up, and it would have the governor's office hit with a lawsuit before a judge could even toss it out of court, because we're still a capitalist country."

Reine dragged her gaze back to Karen. She had a feeling this was likely not the first time they'd argued over what Jack should be doing. She didn't understand a number of laws herself, how they applied and why they had been created. It was a rabbit hole she didn't want to go down.

"Reine, listen. The coverage would have been provided by the fire department. What your husband paid wouldn't have been cheap, so what I can't figure out is why the unions aren't all over this. Did he ever go to his union?"

Reine didn't think she'd ever forget what the union rep had said to her on the phone. The lack of fight from everyone was something she had become too used to. "He said he would send a letter of grievance, but that was all he could do. He told me there were too many loopholes, but while the pre-existing clause was a reach, underhanded, it was something they could get away with."

Karen had an intense way of looking at people, and Reine never wanted to be on the wrong side of her. But she thought she looked tired, too. "You went to the chief at one point. Isn't that what you told me?"

She couldn't remember everything she'd told her. "I did, when I was grasping at anything to keep a roof over our heads, to buy groceries, to just get through the night. I was desperate. He was sympathetic, but he said he couldn't do anything. He made a call while I was there, but he said he'd heard about many firefighters' claims being denied because of pre-existing conditions and loopholes. He told me to get a good lawyer…" She felt so damn awkward, so she looked down to her coffee and took another swallow, keeping her other hand on the baby carrier. Maybe it was the lingering silence that put her on edge.

"Well, you've got one now," Karen stated adamantly. "First I'll draft a letter and send it to this Dominion Group. Damn, I would kill to be able to deliver it in person to the president and see his face when I put them on notice that we're coming after them and will be suing for damages…"

"Yeah, you give it to them, Karen," Suzanne said, her voice fiery. "And don't forget to mention that being a fireman, running in and out of burning buildings, breathing the toxic chemicals he would have been breathing, that was probably why he had cancer. There has to be a report from the doctor?"

Reine glanced to the door to see that Jake was now there, tall, solid. Something about him, his expression, seemed watchful like Marcus, she thought.

"I'm all over that," Karen said. "You let me worry about the legal details. By the time I'm through with them, they'll be running the other way, reimbursing you, Reine, for anything they took from you, issuing a damn apology, and awarding you a settlement. But we will need your husband's doctor's name and your husband's medical files."

Reine nodded. "How am I supposed to get them?"

Karen waved her hand. "You give me his name, and I'll reach out to him for you."

"You're really taking on a lot for me, Karen, and this is really kind, but I can't pay. I don't have any money," she said. She could feel everyone looking at her, and the way Karen lifted her gaze to her, she wondered what she was thinking.

"Reine, I wouldn't take your money if you had it, so stop it, already. We'll make this right. Take a breath, because I can see you've carried this for so long that you probably don't even remember what it was like to be free. And as far as the taxes, the IRS can kiss my ass…"

"Karen, remember what the doctor said," Jack cut in, a warning in his voice. As Karen flicked her gaze up and over to him, something passed between the governor and his wife.

"I am calm, Jack," Karen glanced back over to her and then to her sister and Jake. "My blood pressure wasn't that high at my last checkup, but Jack is hearing only what the doctor said, that added stress is a compli-cation that could put my blood pressure in the danger territory. But I'm not stressed. I'm calm.

"Hey, Jack, you think Harry could handle the IRS thing, by any chance? Put them in a timeout and on hold until we get our pound of flesh from this insurance company and the hospital…" She dragged her gaze over to Reine again. "We're suing the hospital too, and I think we'll add in the union, because with all those dues your husband had to pay, they should have been all over this. I think we'll add in the entire fire department and go after the city of Missoula, too, as well as the mayor and the councilors. After all, your husband was a first responder, a firefighter. They should have had his back."

Reine didn't know what to say. She could see that Karen was ready to go to battle, which could spike her blood pressure and have Jack stepping in and shutting this down.

"Karen…" There was the warning again from Jack.

"Harry is the tax lawyer at the law firm Jack founded, his cousin and senior partner," Karen said. "I'll call him."

Reine looked over her shoulder to Jack, who was staring across the room to Karen, pulling his hand over his face.

"You know I can't get involved, Karen," he said, "but yes, by all means, drag Harry into this. I'm sure he'll handle the IRS. Send your letters to everyone, but I'm warning you, Karen, you're not serving any of them in person."

Karen shot him a smile. Reine knew she was a pit bull, and with the dynamics between Karen and Jack, she thought there was likely never a dull moment.

"You let me know what I can do too, darling," Jake added.

Karen lifted her gaze to Iris's boyfriend, who seemed more like a father to her. Then Reine heard a crash as Cameron ran the big dump truck into the sofa table and knocked over a candle holder, and Arnie let out a wail.

Marcus was in his car, parked behind an older sedan on a side street. The sun had already set, and he was watching Manny Meskill, who had walked to the door of the old fourplex. A dark-haired woman in a brown service uniform had opened it to him, and Marcus wasn't sure what had passed between them, but she had let him in after only a second. Nearly an hour had passed since.

He thought of Charlotte, whom he couldn't figure out how to reason with. He'd never been so far offside before. Then his cell phone started ringing, and his sister's name was on the call display.

"Hi, Karen," he answered without taking his eyes off the rundown fourplex. He took in the city block, the overgrown yard, and the properties around it. Definitely a part of town where people scraped by. On his laptop, he searched the address of the unit Manny had walked into in the police database.

"Where are you right now?" Karen said. The demand in her tone had him pausing.

"I'm working, Karen. What do you want?"

"Really, you mean you're not following that parasite Manny Meskill right now?"

"And how would you know anything about that?" He took in the name that popped up on the screen. The woman who lived in the unit was on parole. "Ah, fuck," he said under his breath, knowing she was likely one of Manny's parolees and he'd been in there too long.

"Suzanne told me, and she dragged it out of Harold. Did you seriously try to imply last night that because I'm pregnant, I'm too useless to help Reine?"

He lifted his hand from the laptop, really listening to the edge in Karen's voice. "That's not what I said, Karen, or meant. I'm very aware of how capable you are, but at the same time, you are pregnant. When you take something on, you go all in and then some. It was concern, is all, that you not put too much stress on yourself. I know what happened before."

There was silence on the other end. He remembered too well that when Cameron was born, Karen had lost her baby.

"You still there?" he said, thumbing down on the mousepad, seeing the mugshot of the woman, Dee Gomez. "And just so you know, I was already put in my place by our little sister, so before you tar and feather me any more, did you get a chance to look into that insurance company? Can they really come after Reine for what looks like interest upon interest and late fees? I'm not a fool. Even I could see the rates were illegal, but somehow they've managed to get away with it."

She sighed on the other end. "It's nothing new, Marcus. It happens too often—and yes, they get away with it, because in order to stop them, you have to have a really good lawyer willing to take on a company with deep pockets and endless resources. They can drag it out for years until they bankrupt you with delays in court and ridiculous lawyer fees that the average person can't afford. Right before the day of the hearing you've prepped for, they ask for another continuance, maybe offer a settlement, until they get the judge they want on the bench. Then the judges have to make a show before siding with the insurance companies because they've been bought off. If you do hold out, half the time they have nothing, no proof. It's just a game of how deep your pockets are.

"Is that what you wanted to hear? Marcus, this insurance company is one of the largest on the west coast, and one of the shareholders is one of the wealthiest men in the country, a major shareholder in too many corporations. The company has a parent company, and profits are probably funneled through a shell company or some nonprofit foundation that funds most of the politicians in office in too many states. Added to that is the money they're making, yet if you really look, like I have, they paid only ninety-three dollars in taxes last year."

He said nothing at first, just absorbing her outrage and fight. He wondered how much of this Jack already knew. "So Reine doesn't have a chance. They really paid only ninety-three dollars in taxes?"

The door of the fourplex opened, and Manny stepped out, tucking his shirt into his pants. The dark-haired woman in a blue robe pulled the door closed. He really was a piece of shit, and Marcus squeezed the phone and stared at the four-door newer Explorer that Manny climbed into and drove away in.

"I didn't say she didn't have a chance, Marcus," Karen said. "Look, she's up against a goliath. Most lawyers won't take them on because of who their shareholders are. And yes, I really did say ninety-three dollars in taxes. I know Jack has been fighting it since he took office. I think everyone would be surprised by that fact that an elite few own many of the big corporations out there. Their foundations are nonprofit, which they use to funnel millions through and pay virtually no taxes."

Marcus could see only the taillights of the Explorer now, and he felt the weight and magnitude of what Karen had said. "It sounds dangerous, Karen, and criminal."

"It is, but it's how the super-rich avoid paying any taxes. The average person out there really doesn't understand that the taxes in this country are completely funded on the backs of the middle class. The super-rich have never paid taxes, because their paid elected officials create loopholes for them, not the people the said asshole politicians are supposed to be looking after."

The street was empty now. "And isn't that Jack's arena?"

He knew his brother-in-law was the governor because of them and his family. He had never wanted it, but a favor had been asked, and he was paying the price.

"Jack isn't a magician. At times, he has to walk a tightrope to avoid descending too far into the rabbit hole our country has fallen down. Those are his words, not mine. There have been too many decades of corruption on top of corruption, and this insurance company is just one more that has been taking advantage of the little guy for too long, because they always pick the ones who can't and won't fight back."

He pulled his gaze, really listening to his sister's voice. "So it sounds like you're on it."

"Oh, I'm more than on it. You know what's better than taking on a giant and winning? Having a whistle-blower on the inside who can provide proof, emails, and the kind of evidence that will be a nail in the coffin for these motherfuckers. I'll expose them for the parasites they are and force them to pay back with interest every dime they stole by denying coverage."

He could hear the fire, the passion, and he knew she wouldn't tolerate coddling. "Does Jack know?"

She said nothing for a second. "You and I both know what Jack knows. I'm the lawyer, and he's the governor. I'm well aware the Dominion Group will paint a picture of political interference and try to have it thrown out because I'm Jack's wife, so from here on out, I cannot discuss this case with him."

Marcus ran his hand over his face, hearing the scrape of whiskers. "Then I guess you have me at your disposal. You'll let me know what you need me to do, what you need help with? And, Karen, anything danger-ous, you let me handle it."

He expected her to yell or say something about how capable she was, but instead she let out a sigh. "Thanks, Marcus. I'll call you tomorrow." Then she hung up.

He stared at the fourplex. The light was on inside, and he climbed out of his police cruiser into the dark-ness, taking in the sounds of the night as he walked up the steps to the door Manny had just walked out of.

He knocked and listened. He heard footsteps and then someone on the other side, and he knew she was looking through the peephole. When the lock flicked and the door opened a crack, he saw the short dark-haired woman.

"Yes, can I help you?" she said. He took in her face and what looked like a slight red swelling of her brown skin just below her eye. It was fresh, as if someone had hit her.

"Sheriff Marcus O'Connell. Are you Dee Gomez?" He could see the fear in her face, in her dark eyes.

"What do you want? I didn't do anything." She pulled the housecoat at her throat, and he nodded. Fear was fear.

"I want to talk to you about Manny Meskill, your parole officer, who left just a few minutes ago."

Her eyes widened. "Did he send you?"

He shook his head. "He doesn't know I'm here. I want to talk to you about him and why he was here for an hour, what he did, and if he was the one who put that mark on your face."

She said nothing, panicked, then stepped back and opened the door wider. "I'm not going back to jail."

He stepped inside. "No, you're not—but depending on what you say, Manny could be."

Nine

There was no family night that day. Eva was coloring on the coffee table in the living room, and Reine could hear Charlotte upstairs with Cameron. The evening had been tense, and so had dinner, as Marcus still hadn't come home.

"Hey, Eva, what are you working on?"

Eva flicked her blue eyes up to her and smiled as she pulled out a shade of green from the box of pencil crayons and started working on the hair of a girl with a dog. "It's a coloring book Alison bought for me. It has all these different dog breeds. You okay, Mommy?"

Damn, she was so sweet and thoughtful.

"Yeah, of course I am. You're quite the artist. You really love coloring?"

Her daughter reached for another pencil crayon, yellow, and kept coloring. "Uh-huh. Are you going to read with me again tonight?"

She wouldn't miss it. She listened to the footsteps upstairs, very aware of how the tension had ratcheted up after Iris left, leaving just the kids and her and Charlotte, silent. Damn, she hated being right.

"You look upset, Mommy. How come you and Charlotte aren't talking?"

She was perceptive, too.

"I think she just has a lot on her mind. Sometimes it's better to give someone some space."

Eva was still coloring, and Reine took in her daughter's hair, the same color as Vern's. She wished Eva hadn't been cheated of getting to know her father.

"That's what Marcus says, too. Do you know when Marcus is coming home?"

She wished she did, because it seemed he was the buffer needed between her and Charlotte. Why did Charlotte hate her so much?

"I don't know, Eva. Maybe soon. Listen, I wanted to ask you about something you said to me this morning."

Eva looked up to her and rested her pencil. Light freckles dotted her face, and Reine wanted to take a second and count them, to burn the image of her daughter into her mind. She was everything to her.

"You remember when we were talking about your grandma and Jake this morning?" She let it linger and could see something in her face and how wide her eyes were.

"I wasn't supposed to say anything," Eva said in a whisper, and that had Reine angling her head and feeling a fury begin to burn deep in her belly.

"I'm confused. What were you not supposed to tell me?" She really looked at Eva and could see the confliction. Damn, what had Marcus and Charlotte done?

"You promise not to say anything? Because Marcus said it was a secret and I can't tell anyone."

"I'm your mother, Eva. You don't keep secrets from me…" She heard the creak of the steps.

"What's going on here?" said Charlotte, wearing a pair of light blue lounging pants with a long-sleeved shirt pulled overtop. By the way she was walking into the room, Reine could tell her mood hadn't improved.

Reine stood up. "Well, that's what I would like to know. What secrets are you telling Eva to keep from me, a secret about Jake?"

Charlotte hesitated. She went to say something, then flicked her gaze down to Eva and said, "Go get ready for bed, Eva."

When her daughter didn't move, Reine could see that wasn't going over well with Charlotte, so she looked down to Eva to see the wide eyes looking up to her. "It's all right, Eva. I'll be up soon, and we'll read that book."

Eva got up from where she was coloring and started walking to the stairs. Charlotte touched the top of Eva's head, then pulled her arms over her chest.

"I love you, but you need to listen to me," Charlotte said to her.

Eva kept walking, looking back once to Reine. She didn't miss the jab. She knew when a woman was threatened by her. After all, she'd spent three years in the best training ground.

When Charlotte looked back to her, she could feel her anger. "We need to set some ground rules, Reine. You need to understand that you're a guest here. You may have given birth to Eva, but I'm her mother. Marcus and I adopted her, and we are responsible for her. I cannot have you undermining my authority."

Sometimes words could be like a punch to the face, and that was exactly what it felt like with Charlotte.

Eva had just reached the top of the stairs, and Reine let her gaze linger on her, then tilted her head and said, "Go on, Eva. I promise I'll be up." She waited until her daughter was gone, seeing the moment Charlotte realized Eva may have heard.

"I'm not sure why you feel so threatened by me," Reine said, "but make no mistake, I will not be a silent observer in my daughter's life. I will not sit by and say nothing or look to you for direction. I appreciate what you and Marcus have done, but don't think you can kick me to the curb and I'll have no say in my daughter's life. Yes, my daughter. I carried her for nine months, I gave birth to her, I love her…"

"You couldn't even keep a damn roof over her head," Charlotte snapped.

Reine had to take a step back, because Charlotte could have slapped her and it would have been kinder. "Well, you're right. I couldn't."

Charlotte shut her eyes, and she could see how bad she felt. Words really could hurt far worse than a beating. "I'm sorry, Reine. I didn't mean it like that." Charlotte gestured to her, then looked over as she heard the door.

Marcus stepped inside and closed it behind him. He watched them as he shrugged out of his coat and tossed it over the rail. "The kids already in bed?" He flicked his gaze up the stairs and then over to them, then stepped into the room.

Reine could see the tension between Marcus and Charlotte. Something else was going on.

"No one going to answer me?" Marcus said.

"Eva is getting ready for bed now," Reine said.

Charlotte turned and walked around Marcus to the

stairs, her back to them. Then she stopped at the foot of them and looked back. "Cameron is still awake if you want to say goodnight to him, Marcus. I'm going to bed."

Then she started up the steps, and Marcus just watched her. He turned back to Reine, and she could see the tension. Husband and wife weren't talking. Another secret? What the hell was going on?

Marcus gestured to Charlotte, who was already up the stairs. "What was that about? I have the distinct impression I walked in on something."

Reine gripped her long-sleeved cream-colored shirt, her arms pulled tight. She had to remind herself that she couldn't walk out the door with Eva. She had no money and no place to go.

"It seems Charlotte is angry with me, and I'm getting the distinct feeling she wishes I weren't here. She certainly doesn't want any relationship between my daughter and me or for me to have a say at all. But I'll tell you what I told Charlotte: Eva is my daughter, and I will not be a guest in her life, Marcus O'Connell. As Charlotte pointed out to me, I know my place, but I will not ask her for permission before talking to Eva, and I won't have Eva be made to feel as if she has to choose."

Marcus didn't say anything. She swore those O'Connell blue eyes could see every secret she had. Then he looked away, crossing his arms, and glanced to the stairs. "Well, I wish she hadn't said that."

She nodded. "Maybe you can answer one thing for me, Marcus."

He gestured toward her and shook his head. "Sure."

"Why are you having my daughter keep secrets?" she said. She could see his confusion.

"Reine, I'm tired. It's been a long day, so I think you need to get to it, because I have no idea what you're talking about."

So he wanted to play that game. She nodded. "Who is Jake, really?"

Marcus stilled and ran his hand over his head. "Jake is my mom's boyfriend. You know that. They live here and in California, where they spend a few months a year."

Yes, that was what they had told her.

"So why did my daughter tell me that you told her not to talk about Jake? There's a secret there, Marcus, and my daughter is not going to keep a secret from me. So either you tell me, or Eva will."

He shook his head. "Not tonight, Reine," was all he said, then turned away from her and started to the stairs. He took a step up them before looking back to her. "Good news on your case. Karen found something."

He kept going up the stairs, but all Reine could feel was that she was the enemy, living under a roof with people she should be grateful to. Yet keeping a secret was dishonest, and it was no different than lying to her. And lying was the one thing, after everything she'd been through, that she could not and would not allow.

Secrets came with a price, and if Marcus and Charlotte asked her daughter to keep one from her, it would cost them.

Marcus had slept on the sofa, evidently, and was just folding the blankets when Reine walked downstairs, dressed, with Eva. There was no way in hell she was tiptoeing around her daughter for Charlotte. The front door opened, and there was Iris, a welcome face, with Jake behind her.

"Good morning, little miss," Iris said to Eva. Reine knew both Iris and Jake had already pieced together that there was trouble in paradise.

Reine heard the stairs creak behind her as she stepped off, and she looked up to see Cameron racing down, yelling, "Grandma, Grandma!"

Charlotte followed him, dressed in her deputy uniform, the same tense expression on her face from the night before. Reine stepped over to the side and let Charlotte pass, and Charlotte let her gaze linger on Marcus before walking into the kitchen, where Eva and Cameron had already gone.

Reine felt a hand on her arm and turned to see Iris's wide eyes.

"Well, I'm going to have a coffee and some breakfast," Iris said. She looked back to Jake, who only tilted his head toward the kitchen, then let his gaze linger on Reine.

"You have a minute to talk?" he said.

Reine blinked, glancing from Marcus back to Jake, wondering what the hell this was. "Sure."

He seemed so kind. He gestured to the living room, where Marcus had finished stacking the pillow on the blanket. She started walking and took in the way Marcus looked over to Jake, whom her daughter was carrying a deep secret about. She stopped in front of the chair and turned in time to catch the exchange between the two men, and her heart thudded, not from fear but from the suspicion that someone was messing with her and her daughter.

"Marcus called me last night about little Eva and a secret she was asked not to talk about," Jake said.

There it was, the anger she couldn't hold back. She dragged her gaze over to Marcus, who didn't look her way, instead giving everything to this man she didn't know, yet she saw he was a very big part of their family.

"Is this where you try to tell me there isn't a secret or that it's none of my business? Let me be very clear with you. My daughter won't be keeping secrets from me." The mama bear in her had her wanting to snarl.

Jake lifted his hands, maybe to calm her, and gestured to the chair behind her, but she'd be damned if she was going to sit.

"If it's all the same to you, I think I will stand," she said.

"Of course. Look, I understand your anger, but this wasn't Marcus's secret to tell."

She flicked her gaze over to Marcus, whose arms were still crossed, and this time he looked over to her and said, "Reine, I don't know how I would feel in your position, if I were in your shoes."

This wasn't making her feel any better, and she wondered if they could tell as much from the expression on her face. "Well, is one of you going to tell me what this is? Because I'm waiting."

She was aware of the voices in the kitchen. Jake took another step, closing the circle between her and Marcus.

"Once upon a time, I had a wife and six children, but I was living a lie because of who I really was and the government I was working for," he said.

She knew she blinked. Finally, she uncrossed her arms and sat down in the chair behind her, then flicked her gaze to Marcus and Jake.

"I had to leave in the dead of night when my children were small and watch them grow up from a distance because that was the only way to keep them safe. I am Raymond O'Connell. Iris is my wife, and Marcus is my son. I came back, but I still had those same people coming after me. The only way to end that and protect my family was for me to die. Little Eva knows who I really am, and she knows she can't talk about me as Raymond or about us as a family. Everyone knows the truth. I'm now Jake from California, Iris's boyfriend. When Marcus called me last night, I knew it was only a matter of time before you would find out. This isn't a secret Eva can keep from her mother."

She had to remind herself to breathe. She looked over to Marcus again, wondering what Eva was in the middle of. "Is Eva in danger?" She touched her chest and leaned forward.

Marcus sat on the edge of the sofa close to her. "No, never. I hope you know that, Reine. The only danger was from the government Dad worked for, but it's fine now because those bad people believe he's dead."

She made herself nod. She had so many questions but couldn't get her mind to focus on any of them. "What kind of government do you work for? What do you do? What is this?"

Jake was still standing, only he wasn't Jake. He was Raymond O'Connell. He was Marcus's father. She could now see the resemblance to his sons and understand the way he was with his daughters.

"I worked for a secret branch of the federal government that keeps an eye on the enemy."

She knew she was nodding, and she dragged her gaze back over to Marcus, gesturing to him mainly because she couldn't figure out what to ask.

"Think the CIA, but a different branch. We never knew Dad was alive," he said. "You were in jail when he reappeared. I didn't set about to lie to you, Reine, and I can't have Eva trying to keep this from you. But at the same time, Reine, you can't tell anyone. I know this is a big ask, and I'm sure you have a lot of questions."

She could hear the phone ringing in the kitchen. The way Marcus was watching her, she realized he was really trusting her with something she could hold over him. "I do have questions, but I just don't know what to ask." She turned to Raymond. "So what do I call you?"

He didn't smile, but the way he watched her, she could see that the O'Connell blue came from him. He had the same eyes, the same expression, as Marcus, Suzanne, Karen, Ryan, and even Owen. She could see it now.

"You call me Jake, just Jake. If you have a question, you come and ask me. But you're part of this family now, and this is a secret we keep as a family…"

"Excuse me," Iris said, appearing in the living room. "That was Karen on the phone. She and Suzanne are on their way over. Reine, you haven't eaten yet."

Damn, she really liked Iris.

"You don't have to wait on me, Iris. I'll grab something. Has Eva had breakfast yet?" She stood up. She'd be damned if she let Charlotte sideline her in her child's life.

"She's eating toast right now," Iris said.

Marcus stood up and walked out of the living room toward the kitchen. Reine now realized there was so much more going on in this family than she had known.

"What's going on with those two?" Jake said to Iris, who had an uneasy expression.

"Oh, I'd say it has to do with me," Reine said. "Charlotte is angry with me, and I suspect maybe she and Marcus are fighting because of it. She feels I'm undermining her with my daughter."

Iris and Jake were both looking at her, yet no one said anything, as Charlotte was now at the door, her coat on.

"Iris, you'll see to it that Eva gets to school?" she said. Her tone was quite abrupt, and she was refusing to look Reine's way as she stared long and hard at Iris.

"Of course we will. You have a good day at work."

Charlotte pulled the inside door open and walked out, then closed the door behind her without a glance back or even a word to Reine.

The moment she left, the tension eased. Jake and Iris

exchanged another uneasy glance and looked back to her.

"I see," Iris said, then gestured toward her like a mother would. "Well, come and have breakfast, Reine. You know, there's one thing about our family you may not have figured out yet. We have disagreements, but when push comes to shove, we do all have each other's backs. Be patient with Charlotte. Evidently, she's hurting."

What was she supposed to say to that?

"Iris is right," Raymond said. "You're Eva's mother, and whether she likes it or not, Reine, Charlotte will see that. Don't worry about her."

Reine took one step and then another as Iris slid her arm around her and walked with her into the kitchen, rubbing her back.

"I'd say come with us to school," she said, "but from the urgency in Karen's voice, she'll likely be showing up with Suzanne before you've had a chance to eat. In case you haven't figured it out already, Suzanne and Karen have taken up arms for you. We're in your corner. So don't worry about Charlotte. She'll come around, and when she does, whatever she may have said, she'll be embarrassed and will likely ask your forgiveness." Then Iris walked around the island and reached for the empty bowl Cameron was drinking his milk from.

Reine looked over to Marcus. The way he leaned against the counter, drinking his coffee, the heaviness lingered over him. He really was carrying the weight of everything. Worse, as she stood there and took in the awkwardness, she realized she might be responsible in an odd sort of way for the wedge that existed between him and his wife.

Eleven

Reine couldn't pull her eyes from the door, where his mom and dad had just walked out with Eva and Cameron.

Marcus was very aware of the bond between mother and daughter. He felt a tap on his arm and looked down to his sister Karen, who wasn't smiling. The way she'd walked through his front door ahead of Suzanne had reminded him of a wrecking ball. She could and would take out anything that dared to become an obstacle.

"So what happened?" Karen said.

He just stared at her, wondering what she was talking about. "With…?" he started, and she let out a sigh. He watched as Reine finally moved away from the door, as his parents had driven away with the kids. Maybe it was seeing her face and the ache she couldn't hide that bothered him so much.

"Where you were last night," Karen said, her voice low. "You know, about that parasite? What did you find out?"

Reine strode into the kitchen with Suzanne. Arnie was fussing again.

"He was visiting one of his parolees and was there for over an hour. She told me that when he told her what he expected from her, she stood up to him, and he had her parole extended an additional six months over a micky of vodka she said he planted."

Karen dragged her gaze toward the now empty hallway. It had taken Marcus most of the night to come down from his blinding rage because Dee Gomez had been reduced to a prostitute for the likes of Manny Meskill.

"You're not saying…"

"You want me to spell it out? He likes to hit women, hurt them. The type of depravity he gets off on would make you sick. Did I get a blow by blow? No. She said she experienced worse behind bars. What that hell does that say about our justice system?"

He knew the many moods of Karen and wondered how much she really understood of what women faced behind bars. He knew it wasn't a cakewalk, but he'd never let himself understand how bad it could be.

"So he uses her for sex and abuses her because he gets a kick out of it," Karen said. "Thank God he didn't get a chance to work Reine. So will she press charges against him? Did you get a statement from her?" She tapped his arm again.

He just stared down at her. She should know how unrealistic that was. "You're kidding, right? And do what with it? Let me tell you about Dee Gomez. She was convicted of fraud, of stealing from her employer, and then lied about it and tried to point the finger at a coworker. Since lying is something she's done, nothing would stick. I know that, and she knows that. It seems Manny picked well, going after the ones who can't fight back. I did leave my card, though. Told her to put it on her fridge and call me when he shows up again. But even if I get him to stop with Dee, how many others is he doing it to?"

He heard the creak of the floorboards and spotted Suzanne and Reine walking in, talking. He wished his wife would be as open as his sisters were with a woman who'd lost her voice.

Karen touched his arm again. "You'll figure something out," she said.

Wow, he hadn't expected the support and compassion. He only nodded and pulled his arms across his chest, knowing he needed to get to work but dreading the cold shoulder from his wife.

"Reine, Suzanne already knows, so I'm just bringing you and Marcus up to speed," Karen said, "but I did some digging on the insurance company, the Dominion Group. I spoke with someone deep in the group who sent me some confidential emails that I don't think anyone was supposed to see."

Marcus just stared at his sister. Did Jack know this? He didn't think so, from what his sister had already said. He sat down on the arm of the sofa as Karen eased herself into an easy chair with a groan.

"What kind of emails?" Reine said. "Is this the whistleblower you were talking about?"

Marcus didn't have to look over to Reine to know the expression on her face was likely one of shock.

Karen did look over to her, though, her hand on her belly. "Her name is Sharron Rowley, and she's an executive with the Dominion Group. When I asked her about your case in particular, after I informed her I was your lawyer, she said to me that it's happened before."

"Wait, are you telling me you called the insurance company that sent a letter to my dead husband denying his medical coverage, and someone just told you that? Like, it was that easy?" Reine flicked her hand to her chest with what Marcus thought was horror mixed with a ton of anger.

"No, it wasn't that easy," Karen said. "I shouldn't be saying this, and Jack can't know, because what I expect is that the Dominion Group could come after Jack. I mean these guys, I'm talking the major shareholders at the top, are the ones in the inner circle who stand with leaders and have been a major thorn in my husband's side. He knew going in what he was up against. Before I made any calls, Jack referred me to Sharron and told me I could use his name. I did, and after talking with her, I knew I couldn't share what she'd said with him, because it could come back on him.

"Needless to say, sometimes a whistleblower has a conscience, and it seems Sharron does. After my phone call, she forwarded me a confidential email from the president of the company that said, and I'm paraphrasing, that profits were down and they should start looking for the easy kills, using a strategy of deny, deny, deny. They were to look at young families, single mothers, anyone overextended with a big mortgage and debts, and avoid anyone who could hire a good lawyer. If anyone fought back with real teeth, they would give them coverage. They used an in-house investigator to compile a list of easy kills... I read enough emails to know this insurance company has a history of denying claims to women whose husbands are terminal and whose families are one step from bankruptcy."

Reine said nothing at first, but she seemed to be thinking some pretty dark thoughts. "So you're saying if I had sold everything we had then and hired a lawyer, they would have just said, 'Oops, sorry, our mistake,' and would have paid for the coverage?" She said it rather calmly.

Karen flicked her gaze up to him, and Marcus wondered how the company could get away with it. Easy. He already knew the answer. "Unfortunately, but that's kind of good news, because after my conversation with Sharron, she also emailed me your case and was going to reach out to the claims department and reopen the file."

"So that means they're going to pay Reine back? It's going to be that easy?" Marcus said. Karen also seemed calm, but he knew that was a ruse. There had to be more. Reine said nothing, just standing there, her hands fisted at her sides.

"No, Marcus, it's not going to be that easy," Karen said. "But I know when I'm talking to someone who can't stand what her company is doing. With enough pressure from me, and if Sharron is wanting to fix the wrongs, she'll put pressure on the claims department. Maybe another letter and demand will need to come from me, but I've already served them with notice of the amount we'll be coming after them for, with damages in the millions. It won't take them long to figure out I'm the wife of the governor. Being a smart company that screws people, they'll know when to cut their losses. So yes, I expect it to be wrapped up shortly, but better yet, I plan on paying Sharron a visit at her house tonight to discuss the case and the other people this company has defrauded."

Marcus just stared at his sister, dropping his gaze to her very pregnant belly. "You said this is a west coast company, so where are you planning on going?" He wondered if she could hear the warning in his voice.

"Relax, Marcus. I'm not going to California. Sharron Rowley and her family live in Billings, not even an hour away. Reine, you up for a road trip?" Karen said.

Marcus pulled his hand over his face.

"Me too?" Suzanne cut in.

"So let me get this straight," Reine said, an edge to her voice. "We're going to see a woman who suddenly has grown a conscience after destroying families?"

He didn't think he could have said it any better than her. He even thought she was about to say no. Good for her.

"Hell, yes," she said instead. "When do we leave?"

What?

"Hey, hang on a second, here," Marcus said. "Karen, I'm not sure this is such a great idea. You don't even know this woman. She's an executive for a major company, yet she's suddenly speaking out? I don't like this. It doesn't feel right…"

"I swear, Marcus, don't let the next words out of your mouth be that I can't because I'm pregnant. I'll have you know I am meeting with Sharron, and I'm getting everything she's walked out of her company with. I'm getting every confidential email, document, and letter that will nail this corrupt company. I will get Reine her pound of flesh, and then I'll find each and every one of the other families that were denied coverage. I don't care if this becomes my only case for the next ten years. This is the kind of corporate corruption I'm not willing to stand for anymore."

His sister could pack a mighty punch. He didn't miss the amused expression on Suzanne's face as she rocked Arnie in her arms, swaying side to side.

"Don't you just love a good fight?" Suzanne said to him.

Reine said nothing at first, then, "Thank you, Karen, but I want only one thing. I want justice for my husband." She flicked her gaze over to him, and he could see a loss that haunted her, one he couldn't imagine, didn't want to imagine.

"I promise you, Reine, they will pay you back every dime, and I'll get you your justice," Karen said. She struggled to slide to the edge of the chair to get up, and he stood and walked over to her, reached for her arm, and helped her up.

"You're not telling Jack, are you?" he said, but he already knew the answer as she stood and looked up at him.

"I can't, Marcus. You know that."

He shook his head. "Then I guess you've got me," he replied. He expected her to say no, but she only made a face.

"Fine. But do me a favor?"

Knowing Karen the way he did, he wasn't going to like this. "And what would that be?"

"You come as Marcus my brother, not the sheriff. Sharron's on the fence, and I likely caught her in a moment of weakness. I don't want to give her a chance to suddenly become scared and backtrack."

"You think she'll realize her mistake and suddenly lie."

Karen nodded. He glanced over his shoulder to Reine and Suzanne, who had turned away and were talking. About what, he didn't know.

"Sharron has come forward and is suddenly honest and forthcoming," Karen said, "but I need to remind myself that she was complicit in this lie, and she participated in taking from Reine and destroying so many other families. She may suddenly have a conscience today, but tomorrow she could realize who pays her salary."

Damn, he hated when she was right. "So no sheriff uniform, badge, or car?"

Karen shook her head. "Nope, just regular everyday Marcus. And remember, not a word to my husband."

CHAPTER

Twelve

Reine had never ridden in a Mercedes. She found herself remembering the Honda minivan her husband had bought new when she'd found out she was pregnant with Eva. It had been a big spend, and the financing had been a stretch.

"You're pretty quiet back there, Reine. Everything okay?" said Suzanne, who Reine realized was the best friend she'd ever had.

"Was just thinking of the house Vern and I bought. It was a small older home on a quiet street, and it had a yard that Vern fenced in with grass, which he mowed every day off. I had flowers planted in the front garden. We weren't rich, but we had everything, furniture, and our cupboards were full. We were even talking about getting a dog before Eva was born, but then we argued over who would train the puppy when he was on shift. We argued about the silliest things.

"So we were looking at adopting an older dog when I came home with Eva to find Vern sitting in the dark brown easy chair he loved in the corner of the living room. He had a lost look about him, and I knew something was very, very wrong. And he told me then: He'd been at the doctor, and they found a mass in his lungs, and it was cancer. I'll never forget that moment, because everything changed.

"The grass got more overgrown the sicker Vern became. He didn't have the strength to mow it, and I had Eva to look after, and Vern, and working. The flowers died. Money was tight, and bills piled up. When Vern died, I had already started selling off everything we had—but the chair… His chair was still in the house when the bank took it. I would like his chair back."

Karen was watching her in the rear-view mirror, and Suzanne, who was tall and slender, turned in the bucket seat. She didn't know why, but she felt she could share anything with her.

"I don't know if that's possible, Reine," Karen said, flicking her gaze back to the road. "I know the money we get won't make up for what you lost, for your husband, and the years without Eva, and the time in jail because you were forced to the streets, but I'll get everything I can."

Reine took in the sign for Billings and the approaching city limits, then looked over to the empty seat beside her. "Do you mind if I ask you something personal?"

Suzanne turned back to her again. "Me or Karen?" There it was, the light-heartedness.

"Well, both. Your mom always takes the kids, Arnie, Eva, Cameron?" she said. Maybe that was what ached, the fact that Reine had never had a mother to lean on with Eva.

"Mom loves her grandkids and is always just a call

away. She looks after Cameron when Marcus and Charlotte are at work, and sometimes Jenny picks up the slack, but we all have each other," Suzanne said.

Reine nodded. "Your family has a secret. Eva told me about your mom and dad—and yes, I know about him. He told me this morning who he really is, Raymond O'Connell, because I lost my temper on Marcus last night when Eva let it slip. I confronted him for the truth. I never expected your dad to show up this morning and tell me."

Karen was looking at her again in the rear-view mirror.

"I know it's a secret, but your dad mentioned something about a government he worked for and how bad people were after him so they have to believe he's dead."

Suzanne looked over at Karen. "We never knew what happened to our dad. He was gone one day when we were kids. He came back just over a year ago. You can't say anything, Reine. I'm surprised my dad told you. Did Marcus ask him to?"

She shook her head, remembering the moment Marcus's cell phone had rung and he climbed from Karen's car before she could pull away. An emergency had come up that he had to handle. "I don't know for sure. All I know is Marcus called your dad. Eva is my daughter, so she won't keep a secret from me. Maybe that's why he told me the truth." She shut her eyes. Her confliction toward Marcus was turning into something she wasn't comfortable with. "No, I won't say anything. Your dad seems like a very nice man. He's been nothing but kind to me."

There was silence again, and she was very aware of how quiet the vehicle was.

"Charlotte is angry with me, though," she contin-ued. "She thinks I'm undermining her with Eva. I told her I will not be a visitor in my daughter's life. I'm her mother. She expects me to ask her permission, I think, before seeing my daughter in her bedroom or spending time with her. I never expected the anger coming at me. You know Marcus slept on the sofa last night? I'm not a homewrecker, but I feel I could be a wedge between Charlotte and him."

Silence again, but she didn't miss the way the energy had changed in the vehicle.

"Charlotte will come around," Suzanne said. "Don't worry about Marcus and her. This entire thing has been hard not only on you but on them. Charlotte just loves Eva so much, is all. Marcus will get through to her. She just needs to understand that you're not a threat to her. Eva has all of us. We all love her."

For a moment, Reine wondered how much she should say. "Aren't I, though? A threat, that is."

As soon as it was out of her mouth, she wished she hadn't said it.

Karen flicked her gaze up to the rear-view mirror and back to her as she pulled up to a set of lights and stopped. "Now, why would you say that, Reine? Families fight, but they make up."

She stared at Suzanne, who was looking right at her, and shrugged. "They do, but I'm not family. I'm the outsider, remember?"

Rather, Charlotte made her feel as if she were an unwanted guest.

Karen gave the car gas as the light turned green. "Don't be ridiculous, Reine. You're not an outsider. Eva is a part of our family, and you're her mother, so that automatically makes you family, as well. Marcus will work this out with Charlotte. She's just hurt, is all. Give her time. You can stay at the condo if you'd like to have some space if things are too tense. We have a spare room, and Jack is already back at home…"

She knew Karen was trying to be helpful, but she couldn't help but say, "I won't leave Eva again."

Karen pulled down the long driveway of a large two-story house with a white SUV parked out front. "Okay, this is it," she said, turning off the car and undoing her seatbelt. "Nice."

Reine stepped out of the back just as Suzanne did, and Suzanne let her gaze linger on her. Reine wasn't sure if she was going to say anything else. Karen started walking to the door.

"So what do we say?" Suzanne asked.

Karen held the deep green painted wood rail and made her way up the three wide porch steps. There was a patio set on the veranda and a porch swing on the end. "Nothing, just let me do the talking," she said as she waddled to the door and pressed the doorbell.

Reine walked up the steps behind Suzanne and wondered if the anger she was feeling was reasonable. She decided to keep that bit to herself.

The door opened, and a woman was there, about Suzanne's height, with short light hair and a square jaw. She was wearing glasses and a black T-shirt over sweatpants.

"Hi, I'm Karen Curtis. Are you Sharron Rowley?"

The woman pushed open the door and glanced back to Reine and Suzanne. "Yes, I'm Sharron. Come in."

Karen went in first. "This is my sister, Suzanne, and Reine Colbert, who is the reason we're here."

Reine closed the door behind her. She took in the spooked look on Sharron's face and the way she didn't pull her gaze from her. There it was, awkwardness. Reine took in the impressive entryway, the high ceiling, and the massive staircase. It was a house she'd never be able to afford.

"Come in, please." Sharron gestured toward them, then walked around Reine and opened the door to look out before closing it and flicking the deadbolt. Reine glanced over to Karen, who had her big bulky purse over her shoulder. Sharron strode past them in pink slippers and led them down two steps into a living room. "Can I get you anything, coffee, tea, water…?"

Reine said nothing as she walked over to a cream-colored easy chair. Karen and Suzanne sat together on the matching sofa.

"Nothing for me," Karen said, and Suzanne only shook her head.

Sharron was wringing her hands. From the sharp and shallow breath she pulled in, Reine could see how nervous she was. Reine took in the mantlepiece, with photos of a family, Sharron with a dark-haired man, smiling, and two teenage daughters.

"I should tell you that I took the letter to the claims department and had them reopen the file…your file." Sharron flicked her gaze to Reine, revealing her discomfort, but Reine couldn't make herself ease this woman's guilt, so she said nothing.

"So is the claim re-opened?" Karen said. "Where are we? Because the emails you sent would be enough for a judge to award a tidy settlement to Reine with interest."

Sharron only nodded. Her hands were linked again

as she swallowed a thick lump. "Well, it seemed good until I received a call from the claims manager, who had your letter and the Colbert file, a thick file. He said legal would have to be called, and anything that was promised now had to be referred upstairs. That was when I was ordered upstairs to the branch vice president's office. He said he would be handling the case, as it needed a special touch, and I was questioned last night about your call. While I was sitting there, he slid across the desk a copy of the email I sent to you and advised me to think very carefully about what my next words were."

Reine felt the rug being yanked from under her again.

Sharron looked over to her, embarrassed. "I'm sorry. I really am," she said. Then she looked back to Karen, awkward, nervous. What the hell was going on?

"So the Dominion Group knows about our conversation, the emails you sent about Vern Colbert?"

Sharron nodded. "And while I was there, the branch vice president received a call from the president, and I was notified that I was being fired for cause. I was walked out of the building and warned of the consequences if I talk to you again. They have all my emails. They've recorded my phone calls, and they've threatened my family…"

She stopped talking and wouldn't look at Reine at first. Then she did. "I'm so sorry. I know what my company did was wrong, but I can't help you. Because if I help you, they'll come after me and my family." Then she stood abruptly and walked to the door.

Reine took in the shock on both Karen's and Suzanne's faces, willing them to do something. Karen started walking, letting out a heavy sigh, and Reine fell in behind her with Suzanne up the steps and to the open front door.

"Again, sorry you came all this way," Sharron said. She reached for Karen's hand, and Karen looked at it briefly, then back to Suzanne and Reine, who followed her out the door and down the steps.

"What the hell was that, Karen?" Suzanne said.

Karen walked to the driver's door, holding a piece of paper, looking around, looking over her shoulder. "I don't know, but she slipped this in my hand." She pulled open the door and awkwardly slid behind the wheel.

Reine closed her door and leaned over the seat, staring at the note Karen unfolded, which read, *Careful, they're watching.*

Thirteen

"Sheriff, you got a second?"

Marcus closed the door of his cruiser, still dressed in blue jeans, a black all-weather, and a red ballcap. He took in Manny Meskill, who was standing on the sidewalk right outside his stationhouse. "What can I do for you, Manny?"

The man had a hard gaze that reminded Marcus just how much he did not like him. "I want to know why you're hassling my parolee. Just what are you up to, anyway? I know you've been following me."

So there it was. He'd expected this at some point. "I don't hassle, but why don't you explain to me what you were doing in Dee Gomez's suite for over an hour? She was in her robe when you left, and her face had fresh bruising. You still like to hit women."

Manny didn't look away. Marcus realized he'd likely been doing this for so long that no one ever questioned him. "Dee Gomez is my parolee, and unannounced visits are the way it works. I don't remember ever demanding you explain your job to me, so I'm not going to explain mine to you. When I pay my parolees a visit, it's never quick. What did she tell you?"

Marcus said nothing for a moment, knowing that unless he caught Manny in the act, he would never be able to do anything for Dee. "Who said she told me anything? But I did tell her that if alcohol mysteriously appears at her place again, she's to let me know. I understand she has four months left on her parole."

Manny breathed in and out but said nothing.

"I expect she'll have no more problems," Marcus continued, "but just to be safe, I told her to call me when you show up again to make sure there are no issues. You see, Manny, a man like you, who likes to hit women, to use them for your enjoyment, is the kind of scum I will make it my personal mission to take down.

"Dee may not be a credible witness. She knows that, and I know that. But we know you've been expecting favors from your female parolees and mysteriously tacking on time for offences when they don't comply with your perverse ways. You're disgusting, Manny. We know now about every woman who has been exploited by you, even the hookers you picked up outside the Rocking Iron. We're watching you."

Manny stepped back, his hands in his pockets, and made a rude sound. "Word of advice, Sheriff: You stay out of my business, and I'll stay out of yours. As far as Dee Gomez is concerned, she has a history of picking up losers. And those hookers are my parolees who are violating their parole. Because I'm not the asshole you're implying, I've given them a warning to get off the streets. You think it's easy, doing what I do, especially with these women? They're magnets for trouble."

Marcus didn't say anything, just stood there, eye to

eye with the man. Then Manny turned and walked over to his SUV. He gave Marcus one last look before climbing in and shoving his key in the ignition.

Marcus only gave his head a shake as a man that disgusted him backed out and drove away. He headed up the steps and walked into the stationhouse, still furious over the call he'd been dragged to, which had turned out to be about missing cattle and should have gone to the livestock association.

When he strode through the door, his gaze went immediately to Charlotte, her round face. Her eyes, which had once softened every time he walked through the door, were simmering still with a hurt he didn't want to see. He closed the door and took in Therese's and Colby's empty desks. Only Harold was at his, on the phone.

"You called me to handle a case that should have gone to the head of the livestock association," Marcus said.

Charlotte stapled papers and flicked her gaze up to him again, then pushed back her chair, walked around her desk to the file cabinet, and pulled it open. "I'm sorry, Marcus, but I made a judgement call."

He stood right behind her and settled his hand on her lower back as she shoved papers into a file. Just his touch had her shutting her eyes, and he knew it affected her. "I was trying to handle something with Karen…"

"And Reine," Charlotte cut in, then slammed the drawer closed and turned around. She was right in his space. He looked over to see Harold watching and slid his hand up his wife's arm.

"Come with me," he said, knowing it came out quite sharply. He pulled Charlotte into his office and closed the door, then let go of her arm. "What is wrong with you? The way you went at Reine, this anger of yours is misplaced."

"Is it, Marcus? I don't think so. She just walked into our house and expects to pick up as Eva's mother. I'm her mother. Reine gave up her rights. This was a mistake. I never should have said okay to letting her move in, but I knew how heartbroken Eva was. I just didn't expect to feel this way, Marcus. I want our family back the way it was, with just you and me and Cameron and Eva…"

He let out a sigh as she paced in front of him. Jealousy, anger. He didn't know how to get her to settle down. "It doesn't work that way, babe. You know that," he said so softly, and he didn't miss her confliction as she stopped pacing.

She walked right up to him and pressed her face into his chest, and he wrapped his arms around her and pressed a kiss to the top of her head.

"We had a family meeting," he said. "You can't go back on your word."

She leaned her head back and pressed her chin into his chest, shutting her eyes for a second. "I know that, Marcus. Just, Reine is just… I was so cruel to her." She stepped back and flicked her gaze up to him. "I didn't sleep well last night. I'm sorry I asked you to sleep on the sofa. Reine will not stay forever, and she's going to want to take Eva with her. I know that. Maybe that's why I'm so freaked out, because I know that Eva loves us, but she loves Reine more. The bond they have…"

He watched his wife, seeing how torn up she was. "Look, Charlotte, I don't know what the future holds, but Eva will always be part of our family. Fighting with

Reine is only going to backfire. You're right. Reine has had to fight for too much. She's not going to leave Eva. I can see that, but right now, they both live with us, and if we get to the point where that happens, then we'll handle it together as a family. But you can't make Eva choose, because Reine will win if you do that. Apologize and work it out. She just wants to spend time with her daughter. Don't make her the bad guy. Be the kind woman I know you are, get to know her, be a friend to her…"

There was a knock on the door, and Marcus pressed his hand to Charlotte's shoulder as he pulled it open to see Harold.

"Sorry to interrupt, but I just got a call from Suzanne," he said. "She said someone tried to run them off the road."

"What, where?" Marcus said sharply. He should have been there with Karen in Billings.

Harold already had his coat on. "Halfway back from Billings. I'm going." He gestured to the door, and Marcus looked back to Charlotte.

She waved toward it. "Go, please…"

He was behind Harold, walking out the door. "Is that all Suzanne said?"

Harold was already pulling open the door of his cruiser. "Yeah. But the woman had been spooked when they got there. She changed her mind on helping them."

Okay, that was exactly what he didn't want to hear.

Fourteen

"So how bad is it?" Karen asked from the side of the highway. Dark was starting to settle in, and the Mercedes was at an odd angle in the ditch. Reine stood behind Suzanne, who was crouched down beside the flat tire. "And how long did Harold say it would be until he gets here?"

Suzanne was squatting, shaking her head, still staring at the tire. "The tire can't get much flatter. Could change it if you have a spare, but we'll never get out of this ditch without a tow. I don't think he'll be long. I'm going to call a tow truck, too." Suzanne really did have a take-charge way about her.

Reine took in the car in the ditch, a steep drop-off, as Suzanne pulled out her phone. Then she walked around the driver's side, where Karen was standing, her hand on the hood, a look in her eyes that Reine was familiar with, scared and pissed.

"Are you sure you're okay? Because we hit the ditch pretty hard," Reine said.

Suzanne was talking to who she hoped was a tow

truck driver, walking back over to the flattened tire and kicking it again.

Karen was standing awkwardly and lifted her hand in a wave. "Fine, just pissed off. Did either of you get the plate of that van?" She was frowning.

Reine was still shaken over what had happened. "I was too shocked. I'm sorry. He came out of nowhere from behind you. Did you see how fast he came up on us? I know this sounds crazy, but I think it was on purpose. He slammed into you, Karen, and drove us off the road."

She didn't want to scare Karen. She took in the driver's side, the scrape of paint and the dent. She lifted her hand to point out the damage and listened to Karen hiss as she ran her hand over her swollen belly.

"I should call Jack," she said. "Damn, he's going to be furious."

Reine didn't know what to make of that. She didn't know Jack well.

"Okay, tow truck is on its way," Suzanne said. "Karen, you sure you're okay? You look a little off."

Karen pulled her hand over her face. "I have never been so scared in my life. Reine is right; whoever that was tried to run me off the road, and all I can think of is that note Sharron handed me. Thinking back now on the moment we stepped into her house, I had a feeling something was off. Scared is scared. Who is watching?"

Reine wondered how big her eyes were, because all of this was because of her, of Vern. What the hell was going on? She heard sirens and looked up, and so did Karen and Suzanne. Then she saw the lights.

"That would be Harold, and looks like Marcus, too,"

Suzanne called out, already on the side of the highway, waving both her arms over her head.

Reine slid her hand over Karen's arm. "Come on, I'll help you up. You sure you're okay? You should call Jack and maybe your doctor, because that was a hard stop. I know my shoulder is feeling a little tight, and you had the steering wheel and the baby."

Karen let out a breath but hadn't moved. Both cop cars were parked now, and Harold was out of the car, talking to Suzanne. Marcus was now walking their way.

Karen took one step and then another, and she winced. "I didn't hit anything, and my seat belt was low enough. I'm fine. But don't worry. Once Jack hears, he'll likely have the doctor over at our house or me in the emergency room with a full workup. Thanks, Reine," Karen said as she helped her up the embankment. Then Marcus was there, reaching for her arm.

"Shit, Karen, what happened? Someone ran you off the road? Why? Were they tailing you, trying to get past?" He pulled Karen up and had his hand on her back, and he glanced over to Reine but didn't say anything to her.

Karen was walking slowly as Marcus led her to his cruiser. She gestured back to the car and said, "My bag. Reine, can you grab everything? My phone is in there, too."

She didn't miss the discussion between Harold and Suzanne, the lights still flashing, as she turned back to Karen's car and headed down the slope, her hand on the driver's door. But all of a sudden, Marcus was there.

"Hey, I'll get it," he said. She only nodded and stepped back as he pulled the door open. "How did Karen get out on this angle? Stand back."

"Suzanne and I helped her out. Marcus, did Karen tell you about the note?"

He pulled out Karen's purse and handed it to her, and she could see by the confusion in his expression that he didn't know. "What note?"

He glanced over his shoulder, and Reine followed his gaze to Karen, who was sitting in the passenger side of the police cruiser. The door was open, and she had a phone to her ear.

"She's calling Jack?" she said, not looking away from her. She felt that unease again with Marcus.

"She's using my phone. Again, what note, Reine?"

She pulled in a tight breath and shook her head. "We were at Sharron's for basically five minutes before she hurried us out, apologizing and walking back whatever she'd said to Karen on the phone. But before we left, she tucked a note into Karen's hand. It said something about someone watching. Who, I don't know, but I have to wonder if this is part of it."

Marcus was now holding Karen's phone, and he gestured toward the incline and took Reine's arm to help her up. "Where is the note?" he said, sounding rather calm, as they walked to the sheriff's cruiser, a car she didn't have fond memories of.

"In Karen's purse, I think."

He reached for it, walking ahead of her and around the open door to where Karen sat, her feet on the pavement, the phone to her ear. She could hear Jack's voice on the other end.

"No, no, no, it's fine, Jack. I'll just stay at Mom's…" Karen said. Then she looked up and let out a heavy sigh. "Fine, I'll see you soon." She hung up. "Well, my officially worried husband is freaking and has the entire entourage coming for me now. Should we wait for the tow truck?"

Marcus handed her purse to her. "No, I'll radio in and make sure they pick it up. I want to see the note."

Karen frowned.

"Reine told me this woman handed a note to you. Now I'm really kicking myself for not coming."

Karen rummaged in her purse and pulled out the folded note, and Marcus took it, read it, and then handed it back. Reine thought he swore under his breath.

"So it isn't an accident, is it? Us being run off the road?" Karen said. Reine found herself reaching for the frame of the door.

Marcus shook his head. "Hard to say, but this, no, I don't believe in coincidence. Okay, let's go. Reine, sorry, but you'll have to ride in the back."

He pulled open the door, revealing the mesh windows and bars of the cramped, uncomfortable back seat.

"I'll ride back there," Karen said. "Reine, you sit up front." She went to stand up and winced again.

"No, Karen, it's fine," Reine said. "I think you should see a doctor."

Karen looked up at her. "Don't worry. As soon as Jack arrives, he'll likely have me in the hospital, being poked and prodded. You sure you're okay with riding back there? I know if I were in your shoes, I wouldn't be."

She really liked Karen. "I'll survive. At least I'm not going to jail, so there's that." She knew Marcus was still standing at the open back door.

Suzanne was now walking their way, Harold with

her, and Karen was rummaging for her phone and dialing.

"Who are you calling?" Marcus said to her.

"I'm going to call Sharron, let her know what happened, tell her to be careful, at least. I'd really like to know who she meant, whoever it is who's watching…" Karen now had the phone to her ear.

Reine stepped around Harold toward Suzanne, who had her arms crossed, rubbing them.

"Well, this didn't turn out like we wanted. Some crazy-ass shit," Suzanne said. "You know, I'm one who doesn't hesitate to run into danger, but this scared the shit out of even me. I guess that's what happens when you become a mother."

"Are you sure?" Karen was saying. "When did this happen? Okay, I'm so sorry." Then she hung up, and maybe it was her tone that had the knot in Reine's stomach tightening again. She was very aware of the cars now going past on the road, the daylight fading.

"What's going on?" Marcus asked.

"Sharron Rowley is dead," Karen said. "That was her husband. He said he found her in the kitchen with a bottle of pills she'd swallowed."

No one said anything.

"I think we should get you back," Marcus finally said. Karen slid her feet into the vehicle, and Marcus closed her door. Reine stood there beside Suzanne as Marcus turned to Harold, a grim expression on his face.

"So Karen was run off the road, and Sharron swallowed a bottle of pills right after you all left." He dragged his gaze over to her, then Suzanne, then back to Harold and shook his head. "No, I don't like this. Something about this doesn't seem right."

Reine looked up at Suzanne, who was looking straight at Harold and Marcus. "Let me get this straight," she said. "Sharron Rowley admitted to Karen on the phone that the insurance company had lied, that they often found a way of denying the claims of people who couldn't fight back. She sent Karen emails, but when we showed up, she was suddenly apologetic, saying she couldn't help me or us. Yet when Karen was at the door, Sharron handed her a note that pretty much said someone was watching. You know, I may not have a college degree, but I can and do question things. How likely is it that this company would do anything to stop Sharron from talking?"

Karen was putting on her seatbelt, and Marcus and Harold were both looking her way.

"I'd say it's not a coincidence," Marcus said. "It's more than likely that Karen has stumbled onto something."

"She still has the emails," Suzanne said.

Reine found herself looking through the windshield to Karen, unable to shake the fear that Karen could be in the line of fire because of her.

Fifteen

The news was playing in his living room. Eva was upstairs with Alison and Cameron, and Reine stood behind the sofa beside Suzanne. His mom was staring in horror at the scene on TV, the news cameras in front of Sharron Rowley's. A byline under the woman being interviewed identified her as a neighbor.

"This is such a shock for the entire neighborhood," she said. "We feel so badly for Greg and the girls, but Sharron has been depressed for a while. She's really struggled with it, and she said once how stressful her job was, how it made her just wish she wouldn't wake up some days. I never in a million years thought she would kill herself. She was found in the kitchen after downing a bottle of pills. This is horrible…"

Marcus took in Jack, who gestured to him from the hallway. He started past Karen, sitting with her feet up on a stool, shaking her head, her eyes glued to the TV. Harold was standing just off to the side as Marcus walked out of the living room.

"Karen's condo was broken into," Jack said. "I just got a call from my security. Whoever broke in trashed it and stole her laptop. I'm taking Karen home tonight."

Marcus felt someone come up behind him and spotted his dad and Harold too. He could hear voices upstairs as well as Charlotte and his mom in the kitchen with Jenny.

"You have round-the-clock security for Karen?" Raymond asked.

"Always. I need to have her see the doctor, as well," Jack said. "You should know that note was just a warning. She's poking into something she shouldn't be. When Karen told me about the company, I did my own digging. Denying medical claims is something this company has a history of. They go after blue collar families. I would estimate we're looking at millions in denied claims."

Marcus felt dampness on his back. "She tell you about the emails from someone inside regarding who to deny coverage to? There are a lot of families just like Reine's," Marcus said.

Jack was neat and tidy as always, with his dark hair and white dress shirt, his sleeves rolled up. "Karen was trying to hide a lot of the details, but I know how the game is played. Emails would be sent to set up the policy for how they could get out of paying. It would be the investigator's job to dig up anything they could use to deny, like in Reine's husband's case, with a pre-existing condition, smoking when he was a teenager. Of course, if they'd fought it with a good lawyer, it would've been tossed out, but the company would have found out everything about Reine and her husband by then—what they owed, what they owned, and how far in debt they were. They would have hedged their bets that the Colberts were living paycheck to paycheck, with a mortgage and no assets, and they wouldn't be able to afford a lawyer."

His dad kept looking over his shoulder. "The suicide was rather convenient," he said, a hard expression on his face.

"Especially for a major corporation like the Dominion Group, whose loose-lipped executive suddenly grew a conscience," Jack said, pulling his arms over his chest. "How do you think they did it?"

Raymond made a face and shrugged. "The note she handed Karen, I'm thinking she was probably told to give it over. I think they were in the house already, and as soon as Karen, Reine, and Suzanne left, they staged the scene. They killed her, put a bottle of pills in her hand. Her family walked in and found her. The news media is suddenly there, along with a convenient neighbor saying she was depressed, her job was too much, yada, yada… It'll be ruled a suicide, case closed.

"The Dominion Group had sealed the leak except for those documents in your condo, so they broke in and stole Karen's laptop. They likely searched your place to make sure there weren't any hard copies, either. Make no mistake that whoever was in there would have known how to get into Karen's computer, access the emails, and walk out with the evidence. With you being the governor, they'll be careful about touching Karen, but that's only if they can find a way for her not to pursue. I guarantee you they'll come back with an apology for Reine now and offer a nice big settlement. They'll expect her to let the rest of it go. But then, she doesn't have the documents anymore or the names of the other families affected. At least Reine will get a new start."

Marcus just stared at his dad, knowing how deep it went. He didn't understand that world and wondered if he ever would. "So is this what you had to do?" he said, though he didn't know why. From the few things his dad had said, working for Mossad, he had participated in the kind of evil he'd said he never wanted near his family.

"There are laws that apply to the average person that do not apply to the top one percent," Raymond said. "Make no mistake, the Dominion Group is part of a larger organization, and these people, these sharehold-ers, have been doing this for a lifetime. They have crooked lawyers who find ways for them to make more money. But there's one rule: You don't talk. Aside from nondisclosures, the company also has something they can hold over their executives. When someone steps out of line or talks, a suicide is the easy solution. Once the husband figures out weeks down the road that this doesn't make sense, his wife will already have been cremated. They'll say it was a mistake, that someone sent her to the crematorium instead of the mortician. They're covering their tracks."

Harold had a certain expression when he was trying to figure something out, but this went way past that. "You think Karen, Suzanne, or even Reine could have trouble coming after them?"

Raymond looked at Jack, and something passed between them. Marcus could hear a phone ringing vaguely in the background, then Karen talking in the living room.

"I'll make a call to Stanley Kassel in the morning," Jack said.

Marcus didn't have a clue who that was, but his dad nodded, and Marcus realized how much of that world his dad understood that he never would. "And who is Stanley Kassel?"

"He's the president of the Beth Kassel Foundation, which holds the majority of shares in the Dominion Group," Jack said.

Marcus realized he might not want to know more. He pulled his hand over the back of his head.

"And one call to him will end any threat to Karen, Suzanne, and Reine?" Harold asked, disbelief in his voice.

"He won't touch my wife because he doesn't want me coming after him or looking into him and what he's really doing," Jack said. "He won't want a microscope on him, his foundation, or any of the businesses funneled through his foundation…"

"Hey, come in here!" Suzanne called out. "Karen is on the phone with the Dominion Group about Reine."

Harold was already walking toward her, and Marcus followed with Jack and his dad. Reine was standing just off to the side as Karen hung up her cell phone and let out a heavy sigh.

"Well, that was the manager of the claims department at the Dominion Group," she started. "Evidently, they would like to settle with Reine."

Marcus glanced over his shoulder as Charlotte, his mom, and Jenny appeared. He could see the open question as Charlotte walked over to him, and he slid his arm over her shoulder.

"It's up to you, Reine," Karen said, "but they offered to pay off the outstanding taxes and reimburse you for all the denied medical coverage, plus four hundred and fifty thousand dollars."

Even Marcus couldn't believe it. He felt Charlotte's hand on his chest.

"That's a lot of money," Reine said.

"You're owed more," Suzanne cut in.

Karen shot her a sharp glance and looked back up at Reine. "Reine, I'll do whatever you want. I'm your lawyer. I can call them back and say no deal, or…"

"Tell them I'll take it," Reine said so softly.

Jack walked over to Karen and rested his hand on the back of her chair. His mom and dad were standing just off to the side, but everyone was looking at Reine, who nodded and then lifted her gaze, first to Suzanne and then to all of them.

"I'm not a stupid woman," she said. "Of course they can afford more, but someone who tried to help me is dead, and you were forced off the road, Karen. I don't want to put anyone in danger. So tell them yes, I'll take the damn four hundred and fifty thousand, because I want time with my daughter. Can you tell them that for me, Karen? And can you tell them that I want them to leave us alone?"

No one else said anything, and he realized Reine understood more of the situation than most would.

"I can tell them that, Reine," Karen said. "And, for the record, I think you've done the right thing."

CHAPTER
Sixteen

"Luke is back," Charlotte said as she walked into the kitchen in a pair of sweats. "Your mom just called. She's not coming this morning."

As Marcus waited for his toast to pop up, Reine was sipping her mug of coffee, sitting on a stool beside Eva, who was eating cereal. Cameron had already jumped down and was running for the stairs.

"So is that why you're not dressed?" he said. "Or are you showing up at the station in sweats today?"

"Ha ha. No, I figure you can get Colby to man the phones this morning, since even Jenny is busy and it's too early for Alison to come over," Charlotte said as she stepped around him to the coffeepot.

Reine gripped her mug and stared down into her coffee. Marcus reached for the toast, which was hot, and dumped it onto a cutting board before reaching for a knife to butter it.

"Reine, are you up to tagging along?" Charlotte said.

He turned, unsure he'd heard her correctly. She leaned against the counter, holding her coffee mug, and Reine appeared as if she didn't know what to say.

"Of course." Her voice was soft, but with an edge.

"Good," Charlotte said. "Eva, are you finished? Because I thought we'd walk this morning. It's nice out and only a few blocks."

Eva finished her cereal, and Marcus could hear Cameron on the stairs again. "I just need to get my backpack," Eva said. She slid off the stool, looking to Reine, who lifted her hand and ran it over her daughter's head.

"I'll go with you," Reine said. She put her coffee down as Cameron slid past them, a ball of energy. "Whoa there, little man."

"Cameron, go get your coat and shoes," Charlotte said. "We're going to walk Eva to school."

"I can put my own shoes on," Cameron said. He had on a pair of jeans and a navy sweatshirt with milk spilled on the front.

"Well, then you go and put them on. You heard your mom," Marcus said. That left just him and Charlotte in the kitchen. He spread peanut butter on his toast. "So what was that about?" He turned to her as he took a bite of his toast, and she looked over to him and shrugged.

"Trying to fix something, I guess. Eva asked me last night why I hated her mom."

Marcus stopped chewing and realized she was serious. He swallowed and shook his head. "And what did you say? Damn, she picks up on a lot."

Charlotte took another swallow of coffee, then put her mug down and turned to him. "It was a wakeup call.

After our talk yesterday, I knew I was going to have to figure out a way to get comfortable with Reine and this…" She gestured around them. "I just never figured I would be called out by Eva. It was on the tip of my tongue to say it was complicated, but Eva wouldn't take that, so I need to figure out how to cohabitate with Reine and make this work."

Marcus took another bite of his toast, hearing voices on the stairs. When Charlotte looked up at him, and he could see her sadness.

"I don't want Eva to leave," she said. "But with the money Reine is going to get, could she get Eva back?"

He pulled in a breath after he swallowed the last bite of his toast and brushed off his hands. "Mom didn't really cancel, did she?"

Charlotte didn't pull her gaze at first. "Luke really is back, but no, I figured a nice walk with Reine and the kids would give me a chance to extend an olive branch, find some common ground."

He heard footsteps and voices at the front door, then took a step toward Charlotte and leaned down and kissed her. "You'd better get going," he said. She made a face when she pulled back. Damn, he really loved her.

"I don't know when I'll be in," she said.

He just lifted his hand as he spread jam on the other piece of toast, which was now cool. "Take your time. And, Charlotte?"

She stopped on the other side of the island, looking over to him.

"This is about Eva first."

His wife only nodded. He could see she was really trying to make this work.

Charlotte shoved her hands in the pockets of her black down coat, and she took in the light blue coat she knew Suzanne had bought for Reine. "That's a really nice color on you," she said.

Reine was walking beside her, holding Eva's hand. "Thank you. It was really nice of Suzanne. Cameron is quite the ball of energy."

Cameron was running just ahead, then rolling in circles on the grass in a couple of the neighbors' yards.

"Cameron, don't run too far! Come on back here," Charlotte called out. "Yeah, he's a handful. Iris said he's a lot like Marcus when he was young. I don't how she did it with six, and she raised them alone through their teenage years, when they got into all kinds of trouble." She could feel Reine looking over to her. Eva really was made in her image. "Eva, do you want to run up ahead and go and bring Cameron back, please?"

Reine gestured to Eva and took her backpack while she ran ahead, calling out for Cameron.

"I wanted to say I'm sorry, Reine, for the other day," Charlotte said. "I truly am embarrassed for how insecure I was feeling and how I came at you. I wish I could take it back." She wondered if Reine would say anything, as she was staring straight ahead, watching the kids, watching Eva. Then she looked over to her.

"You mean it?" she said. Reine couldn't hide how she was feeling.

"I do, Reine. You're Eva's mother, and I haven't been able to figure out how I can still fit in. Marcus and I adopted her because we love her so much, but you're here now, living with us, and I watched as Eva went to you for everything she used to come to me for, and even I'm embarrassed to admit I was jealous and hurt that she wouldn't need me anymore. I was so hurt that I even pushed Marcus away."

Reine was so quiet as they walked. Cameron was now holding Eva's hand, walking back with her.

"So how do we do this?" Reine finally said. "Because I'm not walking away from Eva. I can't be a guest in her life, and I won't ask your permission, Charlotte, to spend time with my daughter. I have no legal authority. I have to look to you and Marcus for that. You know, when my husband got his cancer diagnosis, I thought it couldn't get much worse. But he went downhill fast, and then we struggled for so long to pay the bills, his hospital bills. With the stress of all of it, I never had one moment where I could be happy with Eva without feeling the weight of everything. Ever since I hit rock bottom, being in jail and then separated from my daughter, it seems as if I've always been fighting just to be free."

Charlotte pulled her hand from her pocket and reached over to rub Reine's arm. "I'm sorry if I added to that. I don't hate you. How could I? You're Eva's mother. I hope you won't leave, because I know you'll want to take Eva with you, and I know she'll go, and Marcus and I cannot deny her that even though it would kill us. Eva's family, Reine, but so are you."

Reine frowned and dragged her gaze over to her.

"Marcus and I are her legal guardians," Charlotte continued, "but so are you."

Reine stopped walking and pulled her brows together. "I don't understand."

Charlotte took a step back and stood there, face to face with a woman she hadn't really allowed herself to understand. "Legal parental rights over Eva, Reine. We're sharing them with you."

Reine went to say something, but a tear slipped out, so she turned her head and wiped it away so Eva couldn't see. When she looked back at Charlotte, she nodded, forced a smile, and said, "Thank you."

Reine was still reeling from what Charlotte had said after dropping off Eva at school. During their trip to the office, she had added Reine to the list of who could pick up Eva and had even introduced her to the school administrator as Eva's mother. On the walk back, they'd talked about everything else, Marcus's sisters and brothers and the dynamics of a close-knit family Reine had never thought could exist.

"It looks like you have a visitor," Reine said, gesturing to their house and the pickup out front. She knew the man on the front porch, bulked out, with short hair, had to be Luke, as she recognized him from a photo in the living room.

"Iris said Luke was back. He's the brother in the special forces. Gone one minute, and then who knows when he's back? Hey, Luke," Charlotte called out as they walked up the sidewalk. "Marcus is already gone."

Cameron raced up the steps to his uncle, who picked him up, and the little boy squealed.

"I'm just the driver," he said. "Karen is inside. She

called me this morning and insisted I drive down at dawn to pick her up. Pretty sure when Jack figures out she's back here, he'll blow a gasket."

Reine stopped on the bottom step and just stared up at this man who resembled Marcus in some ways. His eyes were the same color, but they seemed to carry secrets and the weight of something that she understood.

He put Cameron down. "Reine, nice to put a face to the name…"

Charlotte ushered Cameron inside just as Karen walked out in flat boots, a bulky long shirt over maternity knit pants, and a dark jacket overtop. Her hair was pulled up in a messy bun.

"There you are," she said. "Didn't expect to show up here to an empty house."

Reine gestured over her shoulder. "We walked Eva to school," she said, and she didn't know what to make of Karen's face.

"Okay, now you're back. I know we talked last night and you want to take the settlement, but I think you should fight this—and I'll tell you why while we drive. Come on, Luke. Help me down."

Reine just stared in confusion as Luke took his sister's arm and helped her down the steps. "Where are we going?" she said, looking up to him. But he only shook his head as they started to his pickup, Reine following, wondering if this was something Karen did.

"To my condo," she said. "Jack said it was broken into, which pisses me off, and they took my laptop, but there's no way they found everything."

Luke opened the passenger door for Karen and helped her in. Reine knew she was frowning, but she pulled open the back door of the crew cab and climbed in as Luke walked around to the driver's side.

"Karen, you know we were forced off the road, and Sharron is dead," she said. "What they're offering is fine. It won't bring my husband back, but it's more money than I would have ever expected. I'll be comfortable with that and won't have to worry about a debt I can never repay."

Luke started the truck, and Reine reached for her seatbelt and pulled it on.

"Look, I did some digging last night after we got home," Karen said. "That was after Jack insisted my OB make a late-night house call. Hear me when I say I had notes and names Sharron had emailed, and I remembered something Sharron had said to me, that the Dominion Group always went after women like you the same way, denying coverage, citing a pre-existing condition. In each, it was quite a stretch. The medical bills were enormous. The husband died of a terminal cancer, and the wife lost the house. She said something I remembered last night that made me sick. The company execs laughed over the women and kids having everything taken from them."

Luke said nothing, and she wondered if he was even listening as he drove.

"Are you saying there are other widowed women and children who ended up with nothing?" she said. "I was on the streets because they took my salary, my job, everything…"

She didn't want to fight anymore, but Karen looked back to her and said, "It's your call, Reine, but I don't think you should settle, because they're getting off too easy. Those other women may not have suffered the same way, but every one of them did suffer. These assholes knew who to do it to. Too many didn't have the means to fight back."

She turned to look out the window, taking in the familiar streets. "You know, I was really looking forward to this fight being over."

Luke was watching her in the rear-view mirror. "Welcome to the family, Reine," he said. "This is just something you'll have to get used to, because when Karen takes on a fight, she drags all of us in with her."

He parked in front of the condo a few minutes later, and she took in Suzanne standing out front. Reine stepped out of the truck and went to reach for Karen's arm as she slid out.

"You got here fast," Karen called out, and something about the smile between sisters made Reine wonder whether they were partners in crime.

"Well, you did say we're breaking into a crime scene," Suzanne replied, and Reine wondered if she had stopped breathing.

Luke shook his head and held out his hand to Karen. "Keys," he said. "I can't believe you talked me into this."

Karen handed him the keys, and he walked ahead, past Suzanne. She didn't hear what Suzanne said to her brother, but she laughed as he shoved the key in the lock at the front door and pulled it open.

"Karen, a crime scene? Are you kidding?" Reine said.

Karen slid her hand over Reine's arm. "It'll be fine. It's my condo someone broke into. But you know what? I'm not some wet-behind-the-ears girl anymore. I do know what kind of shitheads are out there. The minute I realized what we were up against, with Sharron coming forward, I made copies of what she sent and hid them. Not a chance they would be found. I hid them in a spot no one would find."

She realized Karen was serious as they strode into the building. Luke was already at the elevator, looking around. The elevator dinged, and they all stepped inside, Luke holding the door and pressing the button, still looking around as the elevator started up.

"So what did Jack say when you told him you were coming back here?" Suzanne said.

Luke made a rude sound under his breath. "She didn't tell him. She called me. He likely thinks you're at home in bed, right?"

Karen said nothing at first, and Reine realized he'd just called her out. "He's overprotective. Besides, we're going in and out."

The elevator dinged and opened on her floor, and Luke stepped out first, holding the door until they all stepped out. He started down the hall to her door, and Suzanne fell in behind him. Reine followed with Karen.

There was no crime scene tape on the door. Luke shoved the key in the lock and opened it, then stepped inside first, followed by Suzanne. Reine followed Karen in last when she heard a gasp and spotted a man in black, with a black mask, holding a gun to Suzanne's head, his hand over her mouth, and Luke on the floor, out cold. Another masked man in black was aiming a gun right at Karen's swollen belly.

"Close the door and lock it," was all he said.

Reine froze, taking in the mess of the condo and the fear staring back at her from Suzanne. She closed the door and flicked the deadbolt.

Karen rested her hands protectively over her baby and said, "Who are you and what do you want?"

Luke wasn't moving. Reine didn't know where to look, two men, two guns.

"Karen O'Connell Curtis, seems you angered the wrong person. Wife of the governor or not, doesn't matter. You have something that doesn't belong to you, and one way or the other, we're leaving with all of it."

"You sure it's him?" Marcus said as he took in the flashing lights in front of the cheap motel frequented by hookers. Colby stood outside the open door of room 5C.

Harold fell in beside him. "Yeah, it's him. Maid discovered him this morning. Whoever did it hated him."

Marcus stepped inside the dated, dingy motel room with two double beds, Manny Meskill dead in one. There was blood all over the headboard and the bedspread where the naked man lay, stabbed.

The coroner, an older man in his fifties, Burke Brown, looked over to Marcus after he stepped back so Therese could finish taking photos of the scene.

"Sheriff, looks like he was stabbed about forty times, give or take," Burke said. "Will have to get him back to the morgue, and then I can tell you exactly, but whoever did this was angry. Broke off part of the knife in him. Likely happened sometime last night. Been dead about ten hours, I figure."

Marcus looked around the dive. Manny's clothes were tossed on the other bed, but there was nothing else in the room.

As the coroner stepped out of the motel, Marcus wondered whether he'd ever get used to walking into a grisly murder scene. He turned back to Harold, who was taking it all in. "Any ideas? You talked to the clerk and the maid?"

Harold shook his head. "Yeah. He checked in last night. Seems he's a frequent flyer here. Spoke to the front desk, who said he's here two, three times a week. Pays in cash but stays only a few hours. Hookers, he said. Picks them up, they wait in his car, and then he gets the key."

Marcus had to step out from the metallic odor. He knew he'd never get used to the scent of blood. He stepped out into the sunlight past Colby, who was standing off to the side so no one could go in. A gurney went past into the room with a body bag, and Marcus looked out to the road, knowing Manny Meskill would never get the chance to put his hands on another woman.

"You and I both know what went on here. He's been taking advantage of his parolees, the women, using them for sex. Just took it too far. I guess whoever did this had enough. How far do you want to push this? Because whoever it was just gave every other woman her freedom."

He looked down at Harold, knowing justice didn't work that way. "Start canvassing for her. I know it's not right, but find out who his parolees are, all of them. Get DNA from the room. She'll have left prints, something…"

He glanced to the front office and then back to the open door, where the body of Manny Meskill was being wheeled out, and gave his head another shake. "What a waste," he said.

Harold was walking back into the room.

"And, Harold?" he called out. His deputy turned back to him. "When you find out who did this, make sure there's a deal available, and make sure she gets a lawyer. The thing about men like Manny Meskill is that they get away with this, and these women have to take it. So get a statement from every one of his parolees about how he treated them, how he abused them, and what he forced each of them to do."

Harold nodded. "On it," he said.

Marcus's cell phone rang as he started back to his cruiser, and he pulled it from his pocket, seeing Jack's name on the screen. "Didn't expect to hear from you. So how's my sister today?"

"Funny thing about that," Jack said. "I was in a meeting all morning and just got a call from my security detail that your brother picked her up."

Marcus stopped at his cruiser and rested his hand on the door before he pulled it open. "Which brother?" He winced, noting the sharp edge in Jack's voice, which only Karen could cause.

"Luke. Apparently, she called him, or the other way around. Who knows? But he picked her up after I told her she was to stay home and rest today."

Marcus had to pull the phone away, as Jack had yelled that last bit. "I take it you haven't talked to her?"

"She's not answering her phone. It keeps going to voicemail."

Oh, so his sister was avoiding him.

"You want me to find her?" Marcus said.

"I know where she is. I tracked her cell phone. She's at the condo, you know, the one that was broken into? I'm on my way down to pick up my wife, but I need you to go over there and let her know this has to stop."

Marcus leaned on his cruiser, seeing the open door of the motel, feeling the vileness of the place. Something about it had him wanting to go home and shower. "I'll drive over to her condo right now, but you know very well that Karen doesn't let anyone tell her what to do."

There was silence. He thought he heard Jack swear under his breath.

"I know how stubborn she is. Just go there, and I'm on my way," Jack said, then hung up.

Marcus wondered what was so important that Karen had needed to go back to her condo after yesterday, getting run off the road. He'd seen her face, her fear. Maybe Jack was right. Maybe they all needed to sit Karen down and talk to her about easing up until after the baby, at least.

As he opened the door and slid behind the wheel, the radio buzzed. "Marcus, are you there?" It was Charlotte. So she'd made it into the station.

He reached for the radio. "Yeah, I'm here. So who's looking after Cameron?"

"Alison showed up. Listen, a call just came in, and I thought you should know about it. I heard over the wire that the fire department is responding to a gas leak at a condo building. It's Karen's."

Marcus started the engine and felt a knot in his stomach. An icy chill went right through him. "Are you sure?"

"Positive. Marcus, Karen was at the house with Luke, and they picked up Reine. They didn't say where they were going, but Karen was in one of her moods, you know, when she's ready to slay a dragon."

Damn, and she wasn't answering the phone.

"I've got to go. Call Jack, because he knows she's here, and he just tracked her phone to the condo. Call the fire department and make sure they check Karen's apartment."

Then he hung up the walkie talkie to his dashboard, put the car in gear, flicked on his sirens, and pressed the gas to the floor, his tires squealing. "Damn you, Karen! What the hell have you gotten yourself into this time?"

Nineteen

Reine couldn't move. Her hands were tied behind her back, and her feet too, and the gag from the bedsheet was in her mouth, cutting into her lips. She heard a loud buzzing and knew fire alarms were going off in the building. Karen was lying on her side next to her, her hands and feet tied, gagged as well. She knew this couldn't be good for her, as pregnant as she was.

Luke was still unmoving, and she could see only his feet. She knew the yelling behind her was Suzanne, muffled because she was gagged. As Reine moved and rolled, she could see Suzanne tied to a chair. She knew the smell was from the gas stove, because she'd watched as they'd tied each of them and set down the blowtorch.

One of the men had said, "Found your safe. Don't worry. It will be quick and painless."

The other had turned on the gas burners in the kitchen, no flame, just gas. She stared in horror at them now. She knew what that meant, and she took in the way the condo had been tossed, the papers, the books, the furniture tipped and cushions sliced with a knife, cupboards emptied.

The blast would kill all of them. She hadn't had enough time with Eva. There was no way she could leave Eva now. She was shimmying and rolling, seeing the door. She heard a crash behind her and saw that Suzanne had tipped over in the chair, trying to break the wood her arms and wrists were tied to. She was a mother just like Reine with a baby who needed her.

Karen's face and the tears streaming down it had her rolling and shimmying over to Suzanne, only she didn't have a clue how to get them out of there. How long did they have? Not long. Minutes, maybe?

She reached the arm of the chair, Suzanne on her side, and she heard her yelling through her gag. Reine rolled over and reached behind her, moving closer to her until she could reach her hand, her wrist tied to the arm of the chair. She had to close her eyes to feel for the ripped bedsheet, but it was so tight it was almost impossible to figure out how to untie the knot. Yet if she stopped, that would be the end. She couldn't give up. She dug in with her short nails, feeling the pain as one of them ripped back.

The gas was making her dizzy.

Then she heard the door, the way it splintered and burst open, slamming. There was Marcus and two, three firemen. Damn, she sagged for a moment in relief. She couldn't yell, couldn't get anything out. Her eyes tracked them in their oxygen masks, the one coming right for her.

It was Vern.

Her heart thudded. He looked right at her, his dark hair, his eyes. She wanted to weep. Another fireman went to Suzanne, and she spotted Marcus helping Karen, lifting her and carrying her out the door. Another one had Luke, still unmoving.

She could smell something else. Smoke, she thought. *No!*

Her hands were untied, sliced with a knife, and she was lifted as a knife cut through the rope on her ankles. She was on her feet, reaching for the gag, pulling it down, and she felt dizzy, but it felt so good to be in Vern's arms. He was strong. He always had been. She could just make out Luke ahead of her over the shoulder of another fireman, down the stairs. She hoped Suzanne was behind her.

But Vern had her.

"You came back for me," she said as her heart thudded, picturing Eva and him.

She heard yelling and hurrying down the stairs. *Faster, faster, hurry!* kept going through her head. There was the open door, lights flashing, people and commotion. The arm around her was dragging her along, and she held on to him just as a blast shot out. She hit the ground, Vern covering her, protecting her.

When he sat up and lifted off his mask, she stared at brown eyes, light hair. This wasn't Vern as she remembered him the moment he'd left her. She felt hands helping her up.

"It's going to be okay. You're okay," someone was saying. Then she was sitting on the sidewalk by an ambulance, Suzanne beside her, and oxygen was put on her face. She spotted Karen sitting in the door of the ambulance, holding an oxygen mask to her face, looking up.

When Reine looked up to the top floor, where Karen's condo was, fire burned from the explosion. There would be nothing left.

She pulled the mask away from her face, touched Suzanne's shoulder, and stood and walked over to Karen. Luke was now sitting up on a stretcher, too, touching the back of his head, arguing with someone.

"Are you okay?" she said to him. She felt Marcus's hand on her shoulder, and she looked up to him and back over to Luke, who was leaning over. Someone was pressing a cloth bandage to the back of his head.

He looked to her and winced. "I'm fine. Those sons of bitches blindsided me. I let my guard down." He dragged his gaze to Marcus. "They got away."

She could see he was pissed. "But we made it out," she said to him, then looked down at Karen. "That was too close, Karen. Take the settlement. We have family who need us. I know you want to fight them for what they've done to me and others like me, and I really love you for that, but you can't anymore. You have a baby due, and you have a family who loves you. Let it go."

Karen only shut her eyes. Reine felt the squeeze on her shoulder from Marcus.

"She's right," Luke said. "Now's not the time to fight, Karen. And you know I'll go into a fight anytime."

Karen pulled away the oxygen mask and moved, uneasy. "Are you sure?"

She'd never have believed she could care about the O'Connells as she did now. Damn, they really did have her back. She sat beside Karen in the back of the ambulance and slid her arm around her just as Suzanne stepped over and Marcus pulled her into a hug.

"Thanks for fighting for me," she said.

Karen patted her leg. "Always, Reine, because you're family."

Turn the page for a sneak peek of
THE HUNTER coming next in *THE O'CONNELLS*
Available in print, eBook & Audio

Coming next in The
O'Connells

THE HUNTED

When two prisoners escape and one is found dead, Marcus O'Connell finds himself being hunted—and the hunter could be someone he trusts.

One late night, Sheriff Marcus O'Connell receives a call about two escaped prisoners considered a danger to the community. A search is underway, and the warden has reason to believe the escaped convicts are headed toward Livingston. An urgent warning is issued: Shoot to kill.

Hours later, Marcus is called to a crime scene. The body of one of the escaped prisoners has been discovered deep in the woods, and the scene has already been lit up, with three prison guards standing over the body, along with the sheriff and deputy from the county over and a tracker with his dogs. A story has been neatly put together, and the group at the scene tries to send Marcus on his way.

Yet one prisoner is still missing. Marcus is told no investigation is necessary, that he should sign off on the case and walk away. But nothing adds up. The problem is that dead men can't talk, and Marcus can't shake the feeling that the story he's being told is a coverup for something far more sinister.

The Hunted

CHAPTER 1

The sound of crickets punctuated the quiet neighborhood. Darkness had settled in, but Marcus needed a minute, as he leaned against the large porch beam, before he could lock up for the night and feel that all was okay in his part of the world. He lifted his hand in a wave to his brother Owen and his wife, Tessa, as they drove away in her small compact. Again, he took in the neighbors' houses. Next door, the lights were off and all seemed quiet.

Ryan and Jenny were already inside their house across the road, and the outside light was now off. Marcus waited for that feeling he got every night before locking up, an assurance that it would be okay for him to lay his head down and go to sleep. He counted heads, making sure everyone was okay, listening to the sounds inside his house, the fussing of Cameron, who was doing his nightly protest against going to sleep.

The screen door squeaked open behind him, and Marcus turned to see his dad step out, wearing blue jeans and a black t-shirt. He heard his mom and Reine talking inside. His dad nodded to him and headed over.

"Your mom is finishing up in the kitchen with Reine and Eva," Raymond said. "That boy of yours is just like you. You always fought your mom and argued every night about how you weren't tired, but a second later you'd be out cold. You didn't know how to stop."

Marcus turned to look back at the street. He was still trying to understand his dad. He leaned against the post on the porch, breathing in the warm summer night. The smell told him tomorrow would be another hot day.

"You were rather quiet tonight," Raymond said. "Everything okay?"

What was he supposed to say? This feeling had come out of nowhere. He couldn't remember ever having felt so unsettled, and he didn't have a clue what had caused it—family, life, something else?

"Just one of those days, you know," Marcus said, unable to find words to explain it.

His dad only nodded. It wasn't lost on Marcus that his dad had been forced to stick around Livingston because his mom had refused to leave her children and grandkids. His dad had a way of seeing everything. Marcus had figured that much out, but a stranger wouldn't have been able to tell, as Raymond never let his gaze linger too long.

Now he did, narrowing his eyes, peering out into the darkness. The stars were out, and a few streetlights were on. "Always the sheriff, looking out to make sure everyone is tucked in, safe," he said. "Expecting trouble?"

Marcus looked over to his dad. Inside, the house phone was ringing, and a second later, it was answered.

"You know something I don't?" he said. The sarcasm dripped.

His dad only shrugged. Marcus heard footsteps and pushed away from the post just as the screen door squeaked again, and Reine stepped out, her dark hair pulled back, wearing a peach sundress, barefoot.

"Marcus, it's for you," she said. "It's Therese." She held out the cordless phone.

Marcus didn't look over to his dad, who he knew was watching him in the way only Raymond O'Connell could. Marcus took the portable phone. "Thanks, Reine," he said, then waited as she walked back in the house. He put the phone to his ear, glancing only once to his dad, knowing his deputy called only if there was something he needed to handle. "What's up, Therese?"

"Sorry to call so late, Sheriff, but I have a message from the warden from Montana State. Two prisoners have escaped, and all he said was that they could be headed this way. I was about to call him back…" There was static on the line. His deputy was cutting in and out, as if she were driving.

"Hey, Therese, you're cutting out. You said two prisoners escaped from Montana State?" He was already walking back into the house and taking the stairs two at a time. Upstairs, Charlotte was reading to his son, whom he thought he heard jumping on his bed. Marcus was in his bedroom now, yanking open the closet door and opening the gun safe to retrieve his .357 SIG.

"Sorry, Sheriff," Therese said. "I'm about twenty minutes away, and the cell service is like shit out here. Picked up the message on the way. All it said was that two prisoners escaped. The warden is…"

"Kellogg," Marcus cut in, fastening the holstered

gun to the waistband of his jeans. As he closed up the gun safe, he pictured a man he'd met only a few times.

"I missed that part of the message," Therese said. "I'll give him a call and let you know what he says."

Marcus glanced to the open door. His wife now stood in the doorway. "No, Therese, I've got it," he said. "I'll have Charlotte check the message, and I'll give the warden a call."

She said nothing, and he noted her hesitation.

"Anything else?" he said, realizing it had come out rather short.

"No, that was all," Therese said. "You sure, Sheriff? I don't mind making the call. It may be nothing."

"Or it may be a lot," he said. "No, I've got this one." Then he hung up and held the phone out to Charlotte, taking in her wide eyes.

"What's going on, Marcus?"

He reached for his badge. "Prison break or something along those lines. Therese just called, said the warden at Montana State left a message. Two prisoners. I need you to get his number and play that message for me."

She was already nodding and dialing the office. Something about his wife handling phones and dispatching again settled him in ways he couldn't explain. She scribbled down the number on a pad of paper on the dresser just as his two-year-old son came running in, all smiles, appearing nowhere near ready to go to sleep.

Marcus reached for him and gave him a toss in the air, then held him and kissed his cheek. "Hey, you. Giving your mom a hard time? You're supposed to be asleep."

"Not tired."

"Yeah, well, you will be soon. Go get a book and get in bed."

"Here, Marcus, the number," Charlotte said. "The message is kind of garbled, but yes, it's something about two prisoners escaping."

He put Cameron down after kissing him again and reached for the paper and the phone, shaking his head over his rambunctious son.

Charlotte shook her head. "He's going to be the end of me. You know he argues every night about how he isn't tired?" She pulled her arms over her faded green t-shirt, her dark hair pulled up in a ponytail. "You're heading out, aren't you?"

"Yeah, after I call the warden," he said. "I don't like this."

There it was, that smile of hers he loved. She leaned in the doorway, glancing once over her shoulder down the hall to where their son's bedroom was as he dialed the phone.

"Montana State, warden's office." The voice was muffled, and Marcus had to really listen past the rough twang.

"This is Sheriff O'Connell, from Livingston. Is the warden there? I've got a message from him about a prison escape."

He heard a rustle on the other end, then a clunk. Evidently, whoever had answered barely knew how to use a phone. "Yeah, yeah," the person said, then yelled out, "Warden! Call for you from that Sheriff O'Connell."

Marcus reached for his wallet and stuffed it in his back pocket, then reached for his duty belt. Charlotte didn't look away, gesturing for an explanation, but Marcus only shook his head. There was another rustle on the phone.

"Sheriff? Warden Kellogg here." The man had a deep voice. "Afraid two prisoners escaped. Was discovered only a short time ago by one of the guards. We're in lockdown now. Just finished a count and are interrogating some prisoners. We know two got out for sure, but how, we have no idea. They likely had help from inside. I suspect they could be headed your way. These men are dangerous, both of them. I've already contacted state officials, as well, along with the other sheriffs in the area. An order has already been issued: Shoot to kill."

Marcus angled his head, looking right at Charlotte. He wasn't sure he'd heard the warden correctly. "You can't be serious," he said. "Who authorized that order? With all due respect, Warden, capturing the prisoners is the first priority."

"Sheriff O'Connell, these prisoners are a danger to the community," the warden said. "They will slit your throat and kill you without a second thought. If you want to dance around them and be the nice guy, do it on your own time and not at the detriment of the good people of Montana. You see them, you shoot them, because these two will do anything and everything to avoid capture. Killing, maiming, looting, burning. You want the details of what they'd do to your wife and sisters, everyone in your family, everyone you care about? If you want to argue with me about bringing them in alive, you can do it, but I don't want these two getting anywhere near innocent people. I've already reached out to Judge Harris, and photos of the prisoners have been sent to you."

Marcus didn't have a clue who these two prisoners were or what they'd done, but that sick feeling was back in his stomach with the image of the horror the warden had painted. Damn, what kind of evil had the two men done?

On the other end, the warden was talking to someone else. Then he addressed Marcus again. "Anything else, Sheriff? If not, I suggest you get your ass out there and start looking. Stan has faxed over the photos, and emails have gone out statewide."

Something about Warden Kellogg had always unsettled Marcus, but he couldn't put his finger on what it was. "Yeah, you said they could be headed my way. Why is that? They have family, friends, contacts here? I need all that information."

"Everything about both prisoners has been sent to you. One has a girlfriend, I understand, outside Livingston, and a brother up toward Billings. If that's all, Sheriff, I've got a fucking mess to handle here. You have any questions, get in touch with Sheriff Lester up in Stillwater County. He's got more on them, and he's been on this since word went out. And, Sheriff O'Connell? A word of advice. I understand you may want to give these men a second chance, but sometimes we're all better off if a criminal is six feet under. You understand?"

Yeah, he understood, but a knot twisted in his stomach as he looked over to his wife. He wondered if this explained the sick feeling he had or the cold sweat that had broken out up his spine. "Understood," he said.

"I'll start looking." Then he hung up and tossed the phone on the bed.

"What is it, Marcus?"

Marcus counted the extra clips in his duty belt, then walked over to his wife and ran his hand over her shoulder. "Warden says the prisoners had help from the inside to get out. Says they're dangerous. Photos have been faxed and emailed. Can you access those? I'm going to ask Mom and Dad to stay until I get back," he said. It was just a feeling he had, the need to keep his family together. "See if you can pull up the prisoners' files, too. Warden said they've been sent. I want to know everything about them: who they are, what they did, and exactly how dangerous they are."

He hurried down the stairs, and Charlotte was right behind him. Raymond was back in the house, and he could hear his mom, Reine, and Eva in the kitchen. Marcus stepped off the bottom step, and Charlotte moved around him into the living room, over to the small desk where her laptop was.

"What's going on?" Raymond said as Marcus reached for his sheriff's jacket and lifted it from the hook.

"Marcus, I just sent the photos and files to your phone," Charlotte called out.

Marcus pulled his iPhone from his coat pocket and turned to his dad. "Can you and Mom stay?"

Raymond didn't seem surprised. He only nodded and said, "Yeah, of course. You worried about something?"

Marcus pulled out the keys to his cruiser. "Two prisoners have escaped and could be headed this way. Warden says they're dangerous, so much so that he wants us to shoot first and ask questions later, so I don't want to leave Charlotte, Reine, and the kids alone."

He knew his dad understood. "Yeah, you got it," he said. "You be careful."

Marcus thumbed through his phone and pulled up the photos his wife had sent. One was dark skinned, the other lighter, both with dark hair and brown eyes, the same bugged-out mugshot expressions. Their names were Rafe Jackson and Holter Donnelly. "Charlotte, send these to Harold and Ryan, too," he called out over his shoulder as he opened the door, and his dad was right behind him, holding the inside screen. "Charlotte has the photos," Marcus told him. "Take a good look."

Raymond nodded. "I'll call Ryan and Owen," he said.

Marcus lingered just outside. He didn't know what to say to his dad. Out of anyone, he knew Raymond had a handle on this. "Thanks," he finally said, then started down the steps. He heard the door close behind him and the lock flick closed.

He dialed his cell phone, walking straight for his cruiser and climbing in. As he tossed his duty belt and coat on the passenger seat, the phone rang once, twice…

"Okay, what did you forget?" Suzanne answered. He thought he heard Arnie fussing in the background.

"Put Harold on," he said, shoving his cell phone in the mount on the dash. He started the car.

"No can do," Suzanne said. "He's in the shower. What is it?"

There she went, playing interference. He knew she was still pissed at him because he wouldn't let her play cop in his county.

"You tell Harold to get the hell out of the shower and call me back," he said. "There was a prison break. This is serious shit, Suzanne. Charlotte just sent him the photos and files. I need him to dig into it and then meet me at the office. I'm not messing around. Have him call me. Can you do that?"

She was quiet for a second. "Don't take my head off, Marcus. Yeah, I'll tell him. Hey, big brother?" She always seemed to need to have the last word.

"What?" he said as he backed the cruiser out, ready to get off the phone. He flicked on the headlights and gave the vehicle gas, looking out into the darkness, knowing he'd be taking a second and third look at anyone he saw that night, scrutinizing who they were and what they were doing.

"Watch your back," she said.

He felt a smile tug at the corners of his lips. "Always do," he said. "Now have Harold call me."

Marcus ended the call before his sister could add one more thing. As he rounded the corner, feeling his own angst, he drove slower than usual and took a good, long look at the few pickups parked along the street, scanning for anyone out walking. There was only a couple with a dog.

This was going to be a really long night.

CHAPTER 2

Marcus stood outside the station in the dark, looking right and then left, tracking the headlights of a car as it went by. He heard the distant laughter of a few teens skateboarding just up the block. He was getting a sense for who was out, doing what, and where.

He pulled out his key and shoved it in the lock, then pulled open the door. The hallway was dark, but he didn't flick on the lights as he strode down it, his footsteps echoing. The lights were on inside the county sheriff's office, and he thought he heard voices.

When he opened the inner door, Therese was there, her dark hair pulled back, wearing blue jeans and a gray t-shirt. Colby, the junior deputy, was there too, which Marcus hadn't expected. He wasn't in uniform but instead wore a jean jacket over what he thought was a red t-shirt with a Confederate flag. Both were standing by Charlotte's desk and the fax machine, holding papers.

"Sheriff, the photos and files of the two prisoners came in," Therese said. She held one for Rafe Jackson, the same one he'd already seen. "Colby just got off the phone with Sheriff Lester, who has all his men out looking."

Marcus dragged his gaze over to a quiet Colby. "And?" he said, taking in the young deputy's round face and eyes that were more brown than blue. Colby was lanky and tall, but Marcus still had a few inches on him. He hated this twenty-questions shit, and for a second, he didn't think Colby was going to divulge anything.

"He said not to worry about coming out," Colby said. "He has his men doing a grid search with the dogs, and he told me to pass along that you can stay close to home. They've got this."

Marcus just stared at Colby, then dragged his gaze to Therese. He couldn't shake the feeling that there had been a lot of discussion before he walked through the door.

The door opened behind him, and he expected Harold but glanced over his shoulder to see Suzanne, wearing the same blue jeans and bulky blue shirt under a faded old jean jacket, her long brown hair hiked high in a ponytail. She closed the door behind her.

"Where is Harold?" Marcus said. "Please tell me you're not bringing the baby, too."

Suzanne made a face only she could. "I'll have you know Arnie is at home, fast asleep, and so is my husband. I left him a note."

For a moment, he just stared at his sister, wanting to snap. She'd always been the hardest one to read. "Suzanne, this isn't the time for you to pull this crap. You understand there's been a prison escape? Call Harold. You go home." He knew it had come out rather sharply, but he just turned back to Therese and Colby, who were watching the siblings with wariness. His frustration ramped up as he gestured at Colby. "And what were you about to tell me, Colby? You don't get to talk to another sheriff as if you're running things here. Sheriff Lester has no jurisdiction to tell you to pass along a message like that, as if I shouldn't worry my pretty little head."

"No, Sheriff, sorry, that wasn't what I meant," Colby said. "Or rather, it wasn't what Sheriff Lester meant. I'm sure he was just trying to be helpful, is all."

Now, why didn't Marcus believe that? "So that's it? That was all he said to you? You call him, or did he call here? Because I'm pretty sure my cell phone didn't ring."

Therese was now looking at Colby, and Marcus was starting to sense something else was going on.

Colby looked down to Charlotte's desk and the papers there. "I was here first, and there was a message from the sheriff. I called him, thinking I could get a head start on things before you got here, is all. He told me they're already on it and there's no need for you, that they have all the manpower they need. That's all, Sheriff. He was neck deep, and I could hear the dogs in the background. We didn't talk long."

Marcus glanced back to his sister, who had her arms crossed, watching Colby. She shot Marcus a significant look, and he heard himself let out a weary groan under his breath. He pulled out his cell phone. "I spoke with the warden," he said, "and he figures there's a girlfriend here in Livingston and a brother outside Billings. See what you can find out." He flicked his gaze to Therese, then over to Colby. "Both of you, start digging. What came through on these two?" He took in the message from his wife, a PDF, and tapped it open to see the mugshots of Jackson and Donnelly again, along with their arrest dates, prison records, and next of kin.

"We have a list of misdemeanors for both, nuisance charges, as well as trouble in prison," Therese said, holding out a paper with the same notes that had been on his phone. "Career criminals, by the looks of it. Verbal threats, assault involving a police officer, criminal mischief, unpaid fines…"

Marcus reached for the paper, because Therese had to be missing something, but it was truly just a bunch of petty misdemeanor charges. A pain in the ass, for sure, but not dangerous. The public defender had been the same for both of them, George Wallace, someone he'd never heard of.

"Therese, call the warden back and find out where the rest of the file is," Marcus said. "And call this public defender, Wallace, and find out from him what I'm missing about his clients. We were given an urgent warning, shoot to kill, which is not something I take lightly, and what I'm looking at here doesn't warrant that. I want to know what they haven't told me about how dangerous these two men are. I have a town full of people who have no clue about these prisoners on the loose. If anything, I need an alert put out to everyone in town to be on the lookout. You both got it?"

"Yes, Sheriff, absolutely," Therese said, already on her way to her desk. Colby was still holding some papers, which Marcus snatched from his hands, but they were just a duplicate of the misdemeanor charges, as if someone had just kept faxing the first page.

"Colby, you tell me everything that was said between you and Sheriff Lester?" Marcus said.

Colby looked up at him with wide eyes. "He was just rushed, impatient, is all. Sheriff, he said not to worry, that he's got it."

Marcus glanced back to his sister, who only shrugged and widened her eyes. She thought she was being coy, but he knew her better. He dragged his gaze back to Colby. "Yeah, well, I doubt that. He's got nothing in my part of the county. Go and give Therese a hand." He turned to his sister. "You, come with me."

Marcus headed for his office, hearing Therese on the phone already, wishing Harold were there. He waited as his sister walked into his office behind him, and he flicked on the light and closed the door behind her, holding the knob, taking a second. He walked over to his desk and dumped the papers on it.

"I know what you're going to say, Marcus."

"Oh, I highly doubt that," he said. Everything in his sister's face, her passion, her life, reminded him so much of the little girl who had tried to tag along on whatever he and Ryan had been up to as kids. They'd spent so much time ditching her, and it seemed she was still trying to find a way to sneak in, only now they were grown-ups, and she wasn't scared of anything.

"You don't have to be so nasty," she said. "Besides, you've got Therese and Colby out there, making calls for you. You really should get notice out to the public. You don't have to give details of what they've done, but you need their photos out there so people in the surrounding area know to be on the lookout and not open their doors for a stranger. We don't want someone to take the trash out and find one of these two hiding in their yard. People need to know to lock their doors tonight, Marcus, and maybe keep that shotgun in easy reach."

He just stared at his sister, knowing she was right, but it was only because she was messing with him and interfering in his business, police business, that he wasn't already all over it.

"Don't worry, Marcus," she said as she pulled open the door. "I can handle this for you, and then I promise you I'll call Harold."

He just stared at her. The phone was ringing from Charlotte's desk, and he heard Colby answer it. "Fine," he said. "Handle it. Get the notice out to local TV stations and cell phones, and then you call your husband and go home."

Whomever Colby was talking to, he was now writing something down. "Yes, I'll let the sheriff know," he said. "He'll be right out there." Then he hung up. Marcus had just stepped back around his desk when Colby lifted the notepad and called out to him, "Sheriff, they found them! One's dead, just past Miller's Field. They need you out there to sign off. I can tag along."

Marcus stared at Colby with a sinking feeling. Maybe it wouldn't be such a long night after all. "No, it's fine," he said. "You go on home. I've got this." Then he looked back to his sister, who was giving him that wide-eyed look. He shook his head and said, "You may as well come with me."

There it was, a smile. For a second, he wondered whether she'd do a victory dance.

"Don't get too excited," he said. "Just making sure you don't turn this office upside down."

"Now, don't be nasty, Marcus," Suzanne said, thumping his chest with her fist as she walked past him and pulled open the door.

Marcus glanced back over to Therese, who was now

off the phone. "You too, Therese, head on home. I'll call you if there's anything else," he said.

Then he was out the door behind his sister, letting out a heavy sigh as he took in the paper he held. He knew well the location, a secluded spot in his county. His sister should have been home with her baby, yet there she was, sticking her nose in his crime scene.

"Well, are you coming, Marcus?" Suzanne called from the door and gestured impatiently.

"After this, you go home," he told her. "Better yet, I'll drop you off."

She only angled her head, then gave it a shake and fell in beside him as they walked out to his cruiser. Harold's Kia was parked right beside him.

"You didn't tell Harold, did you?" he said, though it wasn't a question.

Her hand was on the passenger door. Her mouth tightened, and she shrugged. "He really did fall asleep. I left him a note."

He shut his eyes as Suzanne opened the passenger door and climbed in. Yeah, he was going to have to have a word with his deputy about dealing with his sister. He slid behind the wheel and started the car. "When we get out there, Suzanne, I want you to stay out of the way."

"Whatever you say, Marcus," was all she said, and he knew she didn't mean it. Damn, at times, he really did have a ton of sympathy for Harold.

"Lorhainne Eckhart is one of my go to authors when I want a guaranteed good book. So many twists and turns, but also so much love and such a strong sense of family."

(LORA W., REVIEWER)

New York Times & USA Today bestseller Lorhainne Eckhart is best known for writing Raw Relatable Real Romance where "Morals and family are running themes." As one fan calls her, she is the "Queen of the family saga." (aherman) writing "the ups and downs of what goes on within a family but also with some suspense, angst and of course a bit of romance thrown in for good measure." Follow Lorhainne on Bookbub to receive alerts on New Releases and Sales and join her mailing list at LorhainneEckhart.com for her Monday Blog, all book news, giveaways and FREE reads. With over 120 books, audiobooks, and multiple series published and available at all, retailers now translated into six languages. She is a multiple recipient of the Readers' Favorite Award for Suspense and Romance, and lives in the Pacific Northwest on an island, is the mother of three, her oldest has autism and she is an advocate for never giving up on your dreams.

"Lorhainne Eckhart has this uncanny way of just hitting the spot every time with her books."

(CAROLINE L., REVIEWER)

The O'Connells: *The O'Connells of Livingston, Montana are not your typical family. A riveting collection of stories surrounding the ups and downs of what goes on within a family but also with some suspense, angst and of course a bit of romance thrown in for good measure. "I thought I loved the Friessens, but I absolutely adore the O'Connell's. Each and every book has different genres of stories, but the one thing in common is how she is able to wrap it around the family, which is the heart of each story." (C. Logue)*

The Friessens: *An emotional big family romance series, the Friessen family siblings find their relationships tested, lay their hearts on the line, and discover lasting love! "Lorhainne Eckhart is one of my go to authors when I want a guaranteed good book. So many twists and turns, but also so much love and such a strong sense of family." (Lora W., Reviewer)*

The Parker Sisters: *The Parker Sisters are*

a close-knit family, and like any other family
they have their ups and downs. Eckhart has
crafted another intense family drama…
"The character development is outstanding,
and the emotional investment is high…"
(Aherman, Reviewer)

The McCabe Brothers: *Join the five
McCabe siblings on their journeys to the
dark and dangerous side of love! An intense,
exhilarating collection of romantic thrillers
you won't want to miss. — "Eckhart has a
new series that is definitely worth the read.
The queen of the family saga started this
series with a spin-off of her wildly
successful Friessen series." From a Readers'
Favorite award—winning author and
"queen of the family saga" (Aherman)*

Billy Jo McCabe Mystery: *The social
worker and the cop, an unlikely couple
drawn together on a small, secluded Pacific
Northwest island where nothing is as it
seems. Protecting the innocent comes at a
cost, and what seems to be a sleepy, quiet
town is anything but.*

*Lorhainne loves to hear from her readers! You can connect with
me at:*

www.LorhainneEckhart.com
lorhainneeckhart.le@gmail.com

facebook.com/AuthorLorhainneEckhart

twitter.com/LEckhart

instagram.com/lorhainneeckhart

bookbub.com/profile/lorhainne-eckhart

pinterest.com/lorhainneeckhart

In the Silence
In the Charm
Unexpected Consequences
It Was Always You
The First Time I Saw You
Welcome to My Arms
Welcome to Boston
I'll Always Love You
Ground Rules
A Reason to Breathe
You Are My Everything
Anything For You
The Homecoming
Stay Away From My Daughter
The Bad Boy
A Place of Our Own
The Visitor
All About Devon
Long Past Dawn
How to Heal a Heart
Keep Me In Your Heart

The O'Connells
The Neighbor
The Third Call
The Secret Husband
The Quiet Day
The Commitment
The Missing Father
The Hometown Hero
Justice
The Family Secret
The Fallen O'Connell

The Return of the O'Connells
And The She Was Gone
The Stalker
The O'Connell Family Christmas
The Girl Next Door
Broken Promises
The Gatekeeper
The Hunted

The Street Fighter
Finding Home

The McCabe Brothers
Don't Stop Me (Vic)
Don't Catch Me (Chase)
Don't Run From Me (Aaron)
Don't Hide From Me (Luc)
Don't Leave Me (Claudia)
Out of Time

A Billy Jo McCabe Mystery
Nothing As it Seems
Hiding in Plain Sight
The Cold Case
The Trap
Above the Law
The Stranger at the Door
The Children
The Last Stand
The Charity
The Sacrifice

The Wilde Brothers

The One (Joe and Margaret)
The Honeymoon, A Wilde Brothers Short
Friendly Fire (Logan and Julia)
Not Quite Married, A Wilde Brothers Short
A Matter of Trust (Ben and Carrie)
The Reckoning, A Wilde Brothers Christmas
Traded (Jake)
Unforgiven (Samuel)
The Holiday Bride

Married in Montana

His Promise
Love's Promise
A Promise of Forever

The Parker Sisters

Thrill of the Chase
The Dating Game
Play Hard to Get
What We Can't Have
Go Your Own Way
A June Wedding

Kate & Walker

One Night
Edge of Night
Last Night

Walk the Right Road Series

The Choice
Lost and Found
Merkaba
Bounty

Blown Away: The Final Chapter
He Came Back

The Saved Series
Saved
Vanished
Captured

Single Titles
Loving Christine